ALL I EVER WANTED
WAS A PIECE OF CORNBREAD
AND A CADILLAC

ALL I EVER WANTED WAS A PIECE OF CORNBREAD AND A CADILLAC

Bo Whaley

RUTLEDGE HILL PRESS
Nashville, Tennessee

Published in Nashville, Tennessee, by Rutledge Hill Press, Inc.,
211 Seventh Avenue North, Nashville, Tennessee 37219

Typography by Bailey Typography, Inc., Nashville, Tennessee.

Library of Congress Cataloging-in-Publication Data

Whaley, Bo, 1926.
    All I ever wanted was a piece of cornbread and a Cadillac/Bo
Whaley.
        p.   cm.
    ISBN 1-55853-025-8
    1. Georgia — Social life and customs.   2. Whaley, Bo, 1926-
I. Title.
F291.2.W47   1989
975.8 — dc20   89-37922
                                                        CIP

Printed in the United States of America
3 4 5 6 7 8 — 95 94 93

Dedication

To Ludlow Porch,
   the radio thunder that makes Atlanta roar,
and his wife, Diane,
   the lightning behind all the thunder.

Everybody needs a Ludlow and Diane
   to be their friends.
I'm glad I have them for mine
   —two of the best a man could hope for.

Contents

Foreword

I liked Bo Whaley from the first minute I met him. I knew immediately that he was "one of us."

Yes, sir, it was instantly apparent to me that Bo was a bona fide walking, talking, grit-dipping son of these hallowed red clay hills.

And I liked his name. Anybody worth a dipper of pepper sauce knows there have been only a few Whaleys from north of Richmond and no Bos a-tall.

I had been invited to Dublin to speak to The Friends of the Library, and Bo was to act as my host while I was in town. We spent a good part of the evening together. A friendship began then that has grown and deepened every day since.

I guess I'd known him about two years before I read anything he'd written. I was already his friend, but after reading one of his newspaper columns, I became a fan.

When Bo sits down to his typewriter, strange and wonderful things happen. It's hard to explain, but when the rest of us so-called writers gaze at a typewriter, we see only the typewriter and a blank sheet of paper. When Bo rolls his chair to the writing machine, he turns that chair to a seat on the fifty yard line, front row of the passing parade of life.

He sees things that most of us don't notice. He finds humor in old floppy-fendered, ragged pick-up trucks. And wisdom in the lines of a farmer's face. He brings tears to my eyes when he writes about children.

Bo Whaley is first and foremost a storyteller, but he's more than that—much more. When Bo writes about the South, he makes you want to hide behind a Stuckey's and mug a Yankee. When he writes about his youth, he makes you want to splash on a double handful of Old Spice, listen to Hank Williams music, and kiss MayNell Whitlock flush on the mouth just one more time.

All I Ever Wanted was a Piece of Cornbread and a Cadillac glows with the genius of Bo Whaley. It is delicious!

Bo has greatly honored me with the dedication of this book, but far beyond that, he honors me with his friendship.

—Ludlow Porch

Introduction

Have you ever stopped to consider how and where books originate? Frankly, the thought never entered my mind until I began putting this one together.

I'm sure I've always just sort of taken books for granted, giving little or no thought to their origin. Who knows? Maybe publishers have an enormous cave or warehouse filled with yet-to-be-released books, and every year they haul out twenty or thirty or forty and offer them to the reading public. Or maybe they have a regiment of elves armed with hundreds of typewriters in a dark, damp basement somewhere in Brooklyn. When the time comes for a new release, the little men are given six weeks to crank it out, or back they go to wherever ostracized elves go.

And what comes first, the manuscript or the title? In the case of my first six books, it was the manuscript. With this one, the title was born and the manuscript more or less grew around it. Here is a blow by blow, word for word, account of the birth of a book and how it got its name.

The title was conceived at 9:27 P.M., March 16, 1989, at a front table in Annabelle's Restaurant, in Dublin, Georgia, during a conversation that took place between the author and one of his best friends, Ludlow Porch, to whom this book is affectionately dedicated. Ludlow is the popular host of a four-hour morning radio talk show on WSB-AM, Atlanta, and a talented writer and after dinner speaker par excellence. He is also a recognized trivia expert, having been named by *Sports Illustrated* as one of the five most knowledgeable individuals in America regarding trivia.

As strange as it may seem, there were four witnesses to the improbable conception at Annabelle's: Rick Shaw, WSB engineer, who knows more about electronics than AT&T; Donna Canady, a lovely lady now residing in Charleston, South Carolina, who migrated to Dublin from her native Chicago in 1950 and to whom *How to Love Yankees With a Clear Conscience* was dedicated; Ron Pitkin, vice president of Rutledge Hill Press, Nashville, Tennessee, and one of the publishing dynamos who periodically yells down to the elves in the basement (this one in particular); and sweet Diane, who loves, lives, and laughs with Ludlow as his wife.

We had finished dinner and were enjoying coffee. The title was conceived as we marveled over the fact that Ludlow, a giant of a man, had succeeded in losing seventy pounds on a strict, carefully regimented diet. His coat size had diminished from a Ringling Brothers tent to one slightly smaller than a poncho, and he lamented that he'd had to refurbish his entire wardrobe, including the purchase of a new tuxedo for the many formal dinners at which he speaks.

When Ludlow Porch describes a happening, he describes it in great detail. The man could, and would, spend the better part of Leap Year explaining a New York cab ride or what you do with math after graduation, if anything. He described for us the purchase of his new tuxedo and a necessary accessory, a pair of Gucci loafers, the ones that resemble the patent leather shoes worn by the Pilgrims, big brass buckles and all.

"The way I figured it," Ludlow said, "if I was gonna' buy a new tuxedo, I might as well go all the way, complete with the Gucci loafers, so Diane went with me to look at a pair. I tried 'em on, Diane liked 'em, and I told her to write a check for 'em while I looked at some ties hanging on a nearby rack. As I fingered the ties, I heard this voice behind me say, 'That will be $467, Mrs. Porch.' What! $467 for a pair of shoes! I felt like somebody had just unplugged my iron lung!"

Diane confirmed the story of the Gucci loafers and that she insisted that Ludlow buy them.

"I didn't need those Gucci loafers," Ludlow said. "What the heck, I'm just a plain ol' country boy. Just give me a piece of cornbread and a Cadillac and I'm perfectly content."

A book title was conceived then and there. Ron Pitkin's face lit up, and he yelled for a book. This little elf responded.

A thirty-seven day gestation period followed, and *All I Ever Wanted Was a Piece of Cornbread and a Cadillac* was born at 5:42 P.M., Sunday afternoon, April 23, 1989, in the breakfast room of Ron and Julie Pitkin's home in Nashville, Tennessee. An illegitimate birth? Maybe, but you will have to be the judge of that.

Ron and I nursed the child until August 1989, when we released it to go its own way in the world, to travel from Florida to New York, from Texas to Michigan.

Like Ludlow, I, too, am just a plain ol' country boy and *All I Ever Wanted Was a Piece of Cornbread and a Cadillac,* as you will now discover.

—Bo Whaley

ALL I EVER WANTED
WAS A PIECE OF CORNBREAD
AND A CADILLAC

Part 1

Why Me, Lord?

Right off the bat, let me level with you. I'm just a plain ol' small town country boy, but I wouldn't want you to think for a minute that I ain't been around a little bit. I mean, heck, I've dated a real live registered nurse, a waitress on the midnight shift, made the nine ball on the break, drawn a six to an inside straight, sat next to a real live Yankee in a Huddle House once and didn't catch nothin', traveled to Miami and New York and four other foreign countries if Canada counts, been to the Grand Ole Opry, and watched the good ol' boys race at Talladega.

Now that ain't bad for a fella' whose home town is a little place located in South Georgia about 65 miles south of Macon and 120 miles north of Savannah. My town's name is Scott. You can't miss it. It's located on US 80 right between "Don't Litter" and "Resume Speed," and the biggest industry in town is a 400-pound Avon lady who can whip Mike Tyson.

When you drive through, be sure to look for the marker on the side of the road commemorating my birth. I was born in what would be the right front room as you face the house. The sign will be on your right side if you're driving east, and on your left side if you're traveling west. If you're flying? Forget it.

I'm proud of the little sign in front of the old dilapidated and weatherbeaten house that used to be the Methodist parsonage, but is now occupied by rats, roaches, lizards, and a drunk drifter now and then trying to make it to Savannah or Macon, or to the next liquor store—whichever comes first.

I was present for the marker dedication in August, 1982. It was a great day for me. A Notary Public from Willacoochee was the guest speaker, and The Hayloft Boys, a well-known country-western band from Uvalda, Georgia, made music and played my favorite song, "This Old House." Afterward, the ladies from the church served sweetened iced tea and homemade ice cream.

The marker is plain and simple, and I dang near cried when the master of ceremonies took off Jesse Barlowe's KKK sheet that had been covering it for two days and read what was wrote on it: "Hysterical Marker. Birthplace of Bo Whaley, December 11, 1927—or thereabouts."

So much for the marker. What I don't understand is some of the predicaments I wind up in. I mean, I say my prayers, go to church regularly, sit up with the family of the deceased, and buy Girl Scout cookies every year. So, "Why Me, Lord?"

Why do I invariably end up in the women's rest room in restaurants? Get lost with alarming regularity? Get stuck with monumental lunch tabs in spiffy places where they eat lunch rather than dinner, and dinner rather than supper? Get accused of being inebriated when I put on my first pair of bifocals? Fall out of a tree and break an arm while trying to scare a bunch of trick-or-treaters on Halloween? Why do I always end up at ball games sitting next to a know-it-all? Can never find the receipt when I have to return an item for exchange or a cash refund? Go berserk in a supermarket just trying to buy a few items?

I ask you again, "Why Me, Lord?"

What Would Long John Silver Have Done?

I was standing inside a drug store waiting to get to the cashier. I was third in line behind two women who were already engaged in conversation when I joined ranks with them.

"It was terrible. I was embarrassed to tears," one said.

"I'm sure you were. I think that's awful," said the other.

I had no earthly idea what they were talking about. I recalled an embarrassing experience of my own.

It happened in beautiful old Savannah, my favorite city. I was seated in the Pirate's House, anticipating a favorite delicacy, Oysters Savannah. There are times when I dream about Oysters Savannah.

While I love the Pirate's House in general, there is one thing about it I don't care for. I don't like the way their rest rooms are designated. They have these cute little figures of male and female pirates on the doors, but when you're in a hurry who's got time to stop and study figurines? After all, a pirate is a pirate, right? Wrong, Jean Lafitte. It just looks that way.

I placed my order and made my move, easing through a figurine-decorated door and on through a smaller swinging door. You're way ahead of me, aren't you? Ever spent twenty-seven minutes in an isolation booth with both feet shoulder high while making every effort not to breathe? It happened to me at the Pirate's House. Now I know how an astronaut feels.

The moment of truth came when I heard the tap-tap of spiked heels on ceramic tile. Any suspicions I might have had were verified through the female chit-chat over near the mirrors and wash basins. I honestly didn't want to listen, but what the heck do you do when you're only eight feet away? You hold your breath and keep your feet up high, that's what you do. And you ponder and worry, convinced that all your change, comb, fingernail clippers, cigarette lighter, and whatever in your pants pockets will clang to the ceramic tile floor at any moment. You also say a little prayer.

They kept talking and doing whatever women do in front of mirrors and wash basins. Meanwhile, the cramp set in and my thighs knotted up like fishing lines. I didn't dare move a muscle. After all, how would I ever explain this embarrassing headline in the Savannah *Morning News:* Ex-FBI Agent Arrested in Women's Restroom at the Pirate's House.

Lord, I thought they'd never leave! Then panic set in. So what if they do leave and I meet two more coming in as I am tip-toeing out? Sometimes a guy just has to take a chance. And my oysters were getting cold.

I took the gamble and won. I got outside and took a deep breath as a lady approached. She hesitated at the figurine-decorated door sporting the female pirate, not quite wanting to believe she had glimpsed my exit from therein.

She adjusted her bifocals, tilted her head back, and studied the little figurine. Obviously she was no authority on pirate gender, either. "Excuse me, is this the ladies' room?" she asked.

Now calm and collected, along with the self-assurance that she wasn't going to report me to the head pirate, I replied to her inquiry. "I'm not real sure, ma'am. The little figurine on the door should tell you. Is it male or female?"

"Beats me," she said, throwing caution to the wind and whisking past the lady pirate. "I don't know one pirate from another."

Lady, join the crowd.

You say you don't believe this little story? Believe me, I have a witness. I'll never understand how I can get into some of the predicaments I get into. Or how I manage to get out of them.

Oh, the Oysters Savannah? Cold as clams, but delicious.

Not Knowing Directions Can Cause Trouble

First, an admission. I have absolutely no sense of direction, and that can pose a problem at times. It did during my years as an FBI agent, and particularly during the three-plus years that I worked on the underground (or surveillance) squad in Detroit.

It was standard procedure when we had a vehicle under surveillance that I be directed to proceed right or left, up or down, *never* north or south, east or west. During my early days on the squad, I once was told to proceed north to

Flint. I obeyed my order, but after driving for about an hour I saw a sign that read, "Toledo City Limits." And Toledo is southeast of Detroit.

Second, I can't read a map. Can't now and never could. Everything on a map appears backward to me. There is little doubt in my mind that my inability to read a map has a lot to do with my never progressing beyond the rank of Tenderfoot when in the Boy Scouts of America.

I have lived in and around Dublin much of my life, and I couldn't tell you if my life depended on it which way is U.S. 80 west and which is U.S. 80 east. I only know that one will take me to Macon and the other to Swainsboro.

Had I been the navigator on the B-29 bomber that dropped the atomic bomb on Hiroshima, August 6, 1945, there is doubt that New York City would exist today.

I worked in New York from 1962 until 1966 and never knew for sure where I was. On one occasion I encountered a hippie in the Greenwich Village area and asked, "Excuse me, but is that the sun or the moon up there?" He gave me a typical hippie answer, "I don't know, man. I don't live around here."

I have always been big on asking directions when in strange territory. Like one Saturday afternoon, for example, when I was in the vicinity of Douglas. Well, I was really between Denton and West Green, both communities located on highway 221 south between Hazlehurst and Douglas. Got the picture?

It was late in the afternoon, and I needed to locate one Wes Ussery, whose address had been furnished to me as Route 1, Hazlehurst. Now then, Route 1, Hazlehurst could be anywhere from just outside Hazlehurst to the outskirts of Tallahassee, Florida, so I decided to employ my usual tactic. I would ask directions from a native of the area.

You can stir up a hornet's nest by asking directions, and I did. I parked under a big tree, got out of my car, and walked over to where a man was working on the motor of an old model Oldsmobile 442 in his front yard—from underneath. He was up to his elbows in valves, pistons, alternators, and coils, and the only visible clue that a man was underneath the car was a lone bare foot sticking out. So, I talked to the foot—a right foot.

"Howdy," I said to the foot.

"Evenin'," the foot replied while making a quarter turn to the left.

"How's it going?" I asked.

"Rough as a cob," he grunted. "Havin' trouble gettin' this &*#$%# motor mount loose. What can I do fer ya'?"

"Just wonderin' if you can tell me where Wes Ussery lives," I explained as I watched a bare left foot join the right one.

I don't know which foot spoke, but one said, "Yeah, he lives 'bout three miles fum here. Go on down 221 'bout two miles an' turn lef' on the first paved road. Go 'cross th' railroad track an' he lives in th' secon' house on th' lef'."

A strange female voice coming from the direction of the front porch then snarled at my two-footed friend underneath the 442, "He don't neither."

"He dang shore do!" the front yard mechanic yelled back in the general direction of the porch.

"He don't neither," the front porch repeated. "Lives in th' thud 'un. An' th' road ain't paved neither. Been graded, but it ain't paved."

By now two knees had joined the two feet, but the stubborn motor mount still refused to budge.

"I know dang good'n well it is the secon' house, May Nell," the mechanic argued. "Ralph Mitchell lives in the fust 'un and then they's Ussery's house."

"Ain't neither," the porch persisted. "Fust 'un is ol' lady Grimes' house. Ralph Mitchell lives in the second 'un, an' then they's the Ussery house."

I watched the two feet shift, heard the mechanic grunt, and listened. "See, you don' know nuthin'. Ol' lady Grimes died more'n two year ago. An' me'n Daddy was pallbearers, 'member?"

"Wail, jus' 'cause she died don't mean she taken her house with her. Mr. Ussery lives in th' thud house."

"I thought they moved her house to th' river an' made a camp house out of it," the feet and knees chorused in unison.

"Wail, y'cn jus' think agin. I know hits still there 'cause I seen it las' week. An' nother thang, kudzu's done growed up all over it," the front porch said.

"Tha's th' reason I didn' see it then," the mechanic argued.

"Yeah, I reckon . . ."

"Well, I appreciate your help, both of you," I said to the knees, feet, and front porch. "I'm sure I can find it now."

"Wuz ya' wantin' to talk to Mr. Ussery?" the porch asked.

"Right," I said. "I'll go right on out to his house and . . ."

"Won't do you no good," the porch declared.

"Oh? Why not?"

"He ain't home, tha's why."

"How you know he ain't?" the feet and knees demanded to know.

"I know he ain't, 'cause he's standin' right over there 'cross th' road by his pickup talkin' to Mr. Harvey an' Mr. Ramsey."

"Well, dadgummit, May Nell! Why didn' you tell this man that in th' fus place?" the mechanic bellowed.

"Wail . . . 'cause he never ast me, tha's why," the porch said.

I walked across the road and talked to Mr. Ussery. And when I left, the mechanic and his wife were still fussing. And the motor mount still hadn't budged.

Lunch on the Fast Track

I had lunch with a woman executive a while back, complete with subfreezing temperatures as only Atlanta's Peachtree Street can have wind, rain, and snow.

I called the lady, who travels in the upper economic echelon as a senior marketing representative, and invited her to lunch. She suggested "a quaint little place in Buckhead at 12:30. I'll call for reservations."

Ever been to Buckhead? That's where everybody is

either trying to keep up with the Joneses or run over 'em with a BMW, Porsche, or Mercedes with a big number. I'm told that Buckhead women have riding vacuum cleaners, mink dust cloths, with everything from potholders to toilet seat covers monogrammed, and that going to a Buckhead yard sale is tantamount to winning a shopping spree at Neiman-Marcus or Saks.

I knew I was in deep stuff when I arrived at the quaint little place and saw the sign: Valet Parking. I also saw a parking lot adjacent to the place filled with BMWs, Jaguars, Mercedes, a few Lincoln Town Cars and Cadillac Allantes—and a lone Porsche. I turned in to park but was stopped by a fella' wearing a red velvet coat, white jodhpurs, black patent leather knee boots, and a little round black hat, who said, "Sorry, sir. Employee parking only."

He then slid under the wheel of my run-of-the-mill assembly line Cadillac Fleetwood Brougham d'Elegance, dug off like Richard Petty, and left me standing in freezing rain holding a claim check.

I walked inside at 12:27 P.M., checked in with the maitre d', and verified my reservation. "This way, Mr. Whatley," he said as he headed in the direction of a corner table.

"She" arrived at 1:22 P.M., checked her damp full-length mink, and was escorted to my table by the same little fella' who can't pronounce *Whaley* but flawlessly spits out *Gazpacho, Vichyssoise, Ratatouille* and *Chardonnais*.

"Steffan will be your waiter," he said.

Now hear this: female executives run on white wine and get roughly twenty-six mpg (minutes per gallon). Also, they'll eat a crosstie if it's smothered with béarnaise sauce.

We finally ordered at 2:15 P.M., according to her Rolex. Like I said, it was cold and miserable outside and the wine obviously had a warming effect.

I ordered a steak sandwich with stuffed potato. She chose alien chicken with a foreign name that only she and Steffan could pronounce, broccoli with béarnaise sauce, "and another glass of white wine."

The food was excellent, the wine plentiful, and the New York cheesecake delicious. We dropped our monogrammed napkins on the table at precisely 3:25, according to *my*

Rolex, and I signaled Steffan the way I'd seen Cary Grant do it in the movies a hundred times, by nonchalantly lifting a forefinger in his direction. He responded immediately and brought the quaint little check, along with two quaint little foil-covered mints, on a quaint little silver tray.

I felt my American Express card tremble, and at first glance I experienced the same feeling that my friend Ludlow Porch had recently when presented the bill for a pair of Gucci loafers: "$467! I felt like somebody had unplugged my iron lung!" he said.

There it was: $66.36 for lunch! Exactly $9.22 more than the monthly payment on my first house! No charge for the mints. Thank God for small favors.

I was flabbergasted. Heck, I'm a country boy with plain and simple tastes. Just give me a piece of cornbread, my Cadillac, my Rolex, and weekend reservations at the Cloister, and I'm perfectly content.

Facing Up to the Facts

I've heard the expression "There's going to be a rude awakening!" all my life, but I never really considered its impact until I read the headline: Bush Becomes Forty-first U.S. President!

I dropped the newspaper on the table, stared off into space, and realized that I had experienced a rude awakening. I would never become president of the United States. The thought of *not* becoming president had never entered my mind before that moment.

When I was a third-grade student in Alma, Georgia, Mrs. Sarah Tanner, my teacher, said that *any* boy could grow up to be president of the United States. I had no reason to doubt Mrs. Tanner. In fact, I was all set. It was just a matter of waiting twenty-seven years until I reached age thirty-five.

When I was a senior at Stewart County High School in Lumpkin, my social studies teacher, Marion Pugh, repeated Mrs. Tanner's assertion. I believed Mr. Pugh. In 1943, sixteen-year-olds didn't doubt the wisdom of teachers, and I even went so far as to reserve places in my cabinet for the other three boys in my class that totaled but nineteen. The possibility of any one of the fifteen girls becoming president, a policewoman, a bulldozer operator, or a professional wrestler was unthinkable back then.

Once I got to be president, I would name my male classmates to the following positions:

Lawrence Tatum would be my secretary of state. He was the only one of us who had ever traveled out of the state of Georgia, going to Phenix City, Alabama, for his uncle's funeral when he was in the eighth grade.

John Baker would be my secretary of defense. It was an accepted fact that he could whip any boy (or girl) in school, or the night policeman, and had a police record to prove it.

Davis Fort would be my secretary of the treasury. He was the only boy in school who paid for Three-Centas and Johnny crackers with a dollar bill, and any boy who could do that in 1943 *had* to know how to handle big bucks.

It didn't work out. Tatum became a career soldier. Baker became a railroad fireman. Fort became a part-time doctor and full-time cattle farmer.

Me? I went on to more jobs than a migrant worker and lived in more houses than George Washington slept in.

In view of my rude awakening, I've given up on becoming president. I know it's bad to give up on anything, but there are times when we must face reality, and reality is that I ain't never gonna' be president. I know Mrs. Tanner and Mr. Pugh would be terribly disappointed to learn that I've given up, but that's just the way it is.

I've reached the age where I've given up on some other things, too. Here are some of the things I've given up on:
- I've given up on being a millionaire.
- I've given up on traveling abroad.
- I've given up on living in Palm Springs, California.
- I've given up on breaking 70 on the golf course . . . or 80 . . . or 90.
- I've given up on seeing the Atlanta Falcons in the Super Bowl.

• I've given up on seeing the Atlanta Braves in the World Series.

• I've given up on winning anything with a raffle ticket.

• I've given up on being chosen for a *Playgirl* centerfold.

• I've given up on the Alday murderers ever being executed.

• I've given up on attending a concert in a Dublin civic auditorium.

• I've given up on being named to the Ten Best Dressed Men in America list.

• I've given up on bench-pressing more than thirty-five pounds.

• I've given up on balancing my checkbook.

• I've given up on Georgia Power being satisfied with its rates.

• I've given up on syrup and biscuits coming out even.

The presidency? No way. The vice presidency? Well, that's a horse of a different color. I figure if Dan Quayle can back into the job, anybody can. Besides, it's inside work with no heavy lifting and the pay ain't bad. Almost as good as being lieutenant governor, or a member of Congress.

Hotel Lobbies Are Great Places for People Watching

Should you chance to be in Atlanta and have about three hours to kill, I have some suggestions for you. The Cyclorama? Grant Park Zoo? Six Flags? No, none of these.

I was in Atlanta last week to meet a man at the Hyatt Regency Hotel at 6:00 P.M. for dinner and found myself with three hours to kill, having arrived in Atlanta at 3:00 P.M. Here's how I killed the time:

First, I got on I-285. That took care of the first two hours before I finally got off at the East Point exit and somehow negotiated the traffic to the Hyatt Regency garage.

It was 4:53 P.M. when I parked. With an hour to kill, I

went to the lobby, one of the best people-watching spots in Atlanta. I took a lounge chair near the bar, a great seat because 5:00 P.M. is the bewitching hour in Atlanta's hotel lobbies because that's when the convention meetings end and everybody heads for the bar.

I watched the stampede as people poured into the lobby like cattle. *America's crossroads,* I thought as I watched them maneuver for a seat and a drink. The scene never changes, only the faces that rush about in the lobby.

Should you find yourself with time to kill in an Atlanta hotel lobby, here's what you'll probably see and hear:

• The inevitable egghead wearing a pair of those silly looking half-glasses that people always look over rather than through. Conclusion: Anybody who wears half-glasses will probably eat quiche, wear knickers, and smoke rum and maple pipe tobacco.

• The little pot-bellied fella, his pants too long, his coat too short, and the buttons on his shirt in the abdominal area struggling desperately to do their job. The seat of his pants droops to his knees and gives the impression that a large family of Haitians just moved out.

• A pair of myna birds stashed high in the lobby that screech without warning. The screech sounds like the mating call of a hippopotamus or a three-car collision. The initial screech will more than likely scare you out of your Fruit of the Looms.

• Elevators that resemble giant lightning bugs. They scoot up and down, fascinating the kids. Like the one from Willacoochee who was there last week and saw his first elevator. What a shame! He'll return home and live to a ripe old age convinced that all elevators look like the ones he saw in the Hyatt Regency when he was ten.

• Men with briefcases and their wives with shopping bags, the trademark of conventions.

• The convention wit who darts from table to table telling his latest joke or performing his newest magic trick.

• The Casanova, who sits back away from the crowd and studies his prey. Sooner or later he'll decide which woman he will honor this night.

*   *   *

As I sat and watched, I zeroed in on a latecomer, a woman whose arms were loaded down with brochures. Her name tag was crooked and her shoulder bag, about the size of a cotton sack, was hanging on for dear life. She dropped everything on the floor and crashed in the nearest chair. And when I say crashed, I mean crashed. This ol' gal was hefty. She resembled either a large water tank or a small mountain. But what caught my eye was her necklace.

Now, I've seen necklaces, and I've seen more necklaces. But I ain't never seen nothin' like this gal had hanging around her neck. Basically, it looked like it was fashioned from a log chain and had what appeared to be a bronzed bowling ball hanging from it, along with three petrified bananas, several Brazil nuts, four English walnuts, and a chinquapin or two.

Of course, every convention has a sexpot, and I saw her as she walked from the direction of the bank of telephones on a distant wall. When she sashayed through that lobby, even the myna birds hushed. All eyes were on her, and she knew it. She put on a display of strutting and twisting the likes of which I'd never seen before, complete with long platinum blonde hair, red dress split well above the knees, white high heels, and a white shoulder bag monogrammed with the red initials, MBH.

I watched her glide to a table and sit down. She was on her throne, and her subjects were admiring her.

I glanced at my watch. The time was 5:47 P.M. Then, I noticed that the queen, or princess, or duchess, or whatever she was was staring at me. I mean really staring. You know how it makes you feel, don't you? Self-conscious. I'd look away and when I'd look back she was still staring. This went on for about seven or eight minutes until she was joined by another woman. They ordered drinks and lit cigarettes. Then her majesty began staring at me again, whispering to her companion while doing it.

Well, I discreetly checked everything I had on that zipped, buckled, buttoned, snapped, or tied. All seemed to be in order, but she was still staring. I decided right then and there that it was time to make my move, and I did. I rose up out of my lobby chair and marched straight to her table.

"Hello, I'm Bo Whaley from Dublin," I said, expecting to charm her into a trance.

"Hi, I'm Marsha Harwood from Phoenix," she told me. "And this is Rita Patterson from Seattle. I know I must have made you self-conscious by staring at you but . . ."

"Oh, no. Quite the contrary, my dear. I'm flattered. I'd like to invite you to have dinner with me if . . ."

"Oh, thank you very much, but I can't do that," she said. "I'm having dinner with my fiancé."

"I see," I said coldly. "And may I ask why you were staring at me so intently?"

"Well, to tell you the truth, because you look so much like my grandfather," she explained, thereby knocking yet another Casanova off his perch.

The (Not So) Wonderful World of Bifocals

I realize that many of you may not understand this chapter and hope that you never have the opportunity to experience what it is all about—the world of bifocals. As a member of the bifocal club for the past sixteen years, I feel that I can speak (write) with some authority about them.

My initial experience with bifocals came as a lad when I would put on my grandfather's and play like I was in the fun house at the county fair where all those crazy-shaped mirrors make everything, including yourself, appear either ten times too fat or ten times too tall and your face looks like it got caught in an elevator door. It was fun back then because I could take the darn things off and still see. Today, it is quite different.

First, you notice little telltale signs when you hop over the forty mark that indicate you might need to have your eyes examined.

The first big decision is what kind of eye doctor to go to: do you go to an optometrist, an oculist, an optician, an ophthalmologist, or maybe an optimist? After discussing the problem with all your friends and neighbors (who don't know either), you decide on one or the other and get your trusty old telephone book.

Trying to find telephone numbers therein is the prime reason you made the decision to take the plunge anyway. You found out that your arms were about nine inches too short when you extended your arms as far as they would reach while staying attached to your shoulders:

D. Tatched Retina, Optometrist

315 Iris Street :::: 272-1234

By Appointment Only

So, what do you do? You do the same thing that any normal, red-blooded American male would do! You get either one of your 20-20-visioned children or your wife with the x-ray eyes to look it up. You're not about to admit that you're over forty and need a little eye help. No, sir! Not the All-American boy who could spot a miniskirt at five hundred yards and tell right away if she was wearing a wedding ring or not.

With the appointment made and the examination finished (and having failed to read that little Russian's name— RZNFCBOG—that your friend, the optometrist flashed on the wall), you get the word from him in about three weeks when you return to his office to get the glasses:

"Welcome to the world of *bifocals!*"

You leave his office and step (or *try* to step) out into a new world that you never knew existed before, the not so wonderful world of *bifocals!* And, as you stand there on his front steps and prepare to descend from the top of the Washington Monument, you feel certain that everybody is watching you. You cautiously slide your lead foot to the edge of the top step with all the caution of the Great Wallendas on their high wire or a wandering husband trying to negotiate a strange and dark stairway in a hostile neighborhood at five martinis after midnight. Well, you successfully negotiate the first step, and the second and the third fall into place. But then, it feels like the sidewalk just jumped up and met the bottom of your shoe about three feet too soon! And that cotton pickin' line won't vanish from the bottom of your lens! You can wipe, rub, and squint all you please, but the only thing that will erase that line is time, and a lot of stumbles and stumped toes.

Now that you have safely negotiated the steps without breaking the glasses or your neck, it is time to try to learn something over again that you first learned about thirty-nine years before: *How to Walk!* So you just throw caution to the wind and strike out down Jackson Street to your office, or somewhere—anywhere. You give the appearance of a drunken ostrich, wearing skis as you lift one foot and then the other high in the air to step over all those cracks in the sidewalk that look so much like the Grand Canyon. You actually feel, and look, like a forty-year-old fool playing hopscotch on Main Street. Some smart aleck city engineer has raised the curb from seven inches to a disastrous three feet! (The marred and scuffed toes of your previously bright, shiny loafers are evidence of this.) Somehow, by the grace of God you make it to your car and safely home. That's another story.

Later in the evening, while seated with the family for dinner, you try to remain calm and composed as you reach for the salt shaker and ram your thumb and forefinger two inches into the mashed potatoes and then drag your coat sleeve through the gravy as you withdraw your fingers. Of course, you succeed in overturning your water glass with your elbow in the process!

At this point you are sorely tempted to pull off those bifocals and deposit them with your high school class ring, your Second Class Boy Scout badge, and the tassel from your high school graduation cap that hung so prominently from the rearview mirror of your 1947 Ford for years. But you finally settle down and actually succeed in reaching for and getting a roll without turning over your iced tea, or your daughter's who is seated next to you. It seemed that things were going to be all right until your sweet wife becomes enemy number one when she calmly asks:

"Would you please carve the turkey, dear?"

Carve it? Man, you can't even find it! But, you try.

Through the bifocals the thing won't be still, and you aren't real sure that it's dead. You reach out to carve a leg for your starving son and succeed only in snipping off the end of your left index finger. In the meantime, your wife has busied herself in the kitchen; she has no desire to witness the explosion she knows is coming, and does!

With dinner out of the way and having stumbled over two chairs, a toy fire truck, a Persian cat, and an end table, you seat yourself in your favorite chair with the newspaper, ready to reap some of the benefits from those bifocal monsters. You hold your head back and try to adjust it and the paper so that both fit into those little inserts called bifocals. It doesn't work. Either your head is too far back, or you are holding the paper too low. It doesn't help at all when your son makes his ill-timed statement, "What's the matter, Daddy? You got a crick in your neck?"

You don't answer, but the look you flash back at him would melt an Alaskan iceberg! Mama knows better. She just takes her time doing the dishes while your daughter cleans the tablecloth.

You finally give up on the paper and opt for a little TV before retiring. No sale, Big Daddy! You again rear your head back as you squat in front of the tube and try to find Channel 5 only to find that 5, 2, 7, and 4 all look alike through the bifocals. So off you go to bed. Your prayer that night will surely be that should you dream, you might be spared the agony of dreaming through bifocals!

How to Spot New Bifocal Victims

1. Observe the earlobes; they will be nicked and scraped from shaving.

2. Check the area around the gas tank nozzle on his car trunk lid. You will notice numerous dents and scratches in a circle about ten inches in circumference (since the advent of self-service gas).

3. Watch him try to read his watch . . . and then turn to the first person available and ask, "You got the time? I think my watch has stopped." (It did, the day he slapped on the bifocals!)

4. Observe him closely as he attempts to unlock the car

door or put the key in the ignition. It is during those trying times that old Dad reverts to his boyhood days at grandfather's house and the pin the tail on the donkey game.

He will receive one instant benefit from his newly acquired bifocals, though. When he gets the bill from his eye doctor, he won't be able to read it!

There's No Fool Like an Old Fool

My Saturday was going great, although my golf game wasn't. After finishing eighteen holes, I headed home to shower and shave before going to see my best girl. I took her to Swampland for catfish.

Afterward, we drove back to "her" house. A definite mistake. Why? Her daughter was there with her boyfriend and greeted us at the door with what they called a great idea.

"Bo! Let's all go roller skating!" she threw at me with absolutely no warning.

"Great idea!" her boyfriend chimed in. Well, why wouldn't he? The son-of-a-gun jumps out of airplanes for relaxation.

I didn't panic because I knew "she" would catch on and go along with my reply.

"Naw, I'm sure your mother would rather stay home and watch TV."

"She" killed that remark deader than King Tut.

"Yeah. I'd love it. Let's go!" she said.

Soooooo, off we went.

I hadn't skated since the days when you slid the toes of your shoes through the adjustable clamps and twisted the skate key to tighten them until the toes of your shoes resembled two pregnant shrimp.

Skating rinks? They were in such far away places as Chicago, Los Angeles, Detroit, and Macon. Those of us who skated on sidewalks in places like Oglethorpe, Alma, and Lumpkin had never seen one. Shoe skates? They only existed in Sears, Roebuck and Montgomery Ward catalogues.

Ours were all the same brand, Union Hardware, complete with toe clamps and skate key.

I could never find the cotton pickin' key. But, you know what I did, don't you? Sure you do, I slipped my daddy's pliers out of his tool box. After using them on the toe clamps a few times, the key wouldn't work anyway.

Ever try to borrow a skate key from a girl? Forget it! They always had it hanging around their necks, and borrowing a skate key from a girl right in front of everybody was almost equal to becoming engaged. It's like that when you're thirteen, going on fourteen. And what boy in his right mind would tighten his skates with a skate key on a pink ribbon? Only as a last resort, if I couldn't find the pliers.

Roller skating on a Saturday night? I tried it. For me jumping out of airplanes is safer. But what do you do when your best girl is watching? Heck, I'm too old to do cartwheels and somersaults. I gave it my best shot and damn near broke my neck!

After lacing on a pair of those four-wheel drives, I was off to the races. Man, did I ever put on a show! And at age fifty-three.

My first trick was to stand up, a monumental achievement. Next, I shuffled off in the beginner's area toward a distant wall. Unable to stop, I plowed over a nine-year-old boy, twisted and turned on one skate while imitating a drunken Indian war dancer, and knocked a six-year-old to his knees before whizzing through the door to the men's room.

What else could I say? "Sorry about that, but when you gotta' go you gotta' go!" I shouted.

I finally emerged from my hideaway and made it to the main arena. Off I skated, round and round, going through more maneuvers than a kid playing hopscotch. Maneuvers? Peggy Fleming should be so graceful.

I could hear the comments from the fellow skaters above the strains of the music.

"Look at him, Daddy! He's skating on one foot, backward!" "Hey, did you see that? The old guy just did a double twisting turn and shoulder-high leg kick." "Mommy! Mommy! Look at the funny man doing a split! He's good!"

Good? No way, sugar. *Dumb* is the word.

Split? Wrong again. The correct word for the maneuver is *hernia*.

I heard her call out in a loud voice as I bent double, dying.

"Do it again, mister! Do it again!"

I did one better than that. For my finale I gave my best impersonation of a drunken sailor aboard a steel-decked ship trying desperately to move from the bow to the stern on roller skates in the midst of Hurricane David while sending semaphore SOS hand signals to the heavens.

Miraculously, I made it to the bench, collapsed, and removed the four-wheel drives, convinced beyond any doubt that man was not designed to walk on wheels.

When I returned the skates to the rental desk, the nice lady smiled and said, "Man, you were great out there! Some of us were just saying that in your younger days you must have been a professional."

I smiled, thanked her, and walked away on two legs that in less than an hour had been transformed to railroad ties, complete with spikes and nails. For good measure, I was nursing a double hernia, two blistered toes, and sporting a ripped pair of Jaymar trousers.

"You done good, Bo. You done good," "she" said as I hobbled through the parking lot.

Isn't it amazing what a boy—no matter what age—will go through to impress a girl?

The Old Trick or Treat(ment)

Warning: Bo Whaley has determined that trick or treating may be hazardous to your health!

How do I know that? Well, friend, I've been down the road, up the tree, and down the tree with Halloween shenanigans. Lend an ear. What I relate to you now is the truth, the whole truth, and nothing but the truth.

* * *

It happened in Swainsboro in October 1967, Halloween night. It was a most memorable night(mare).

My new house had just been completed. The furniture was all in place. In the garage, seemingly hundreds of "things" were piled, stacked, or thrown, awaiting their final destination. But it was Halloween and no time to worry about such garage sale material as a broken wagon, 300 old books, a Japanese helmet of World War II vintage, a dead television set, a dying clock radio, and a pile of mixed treasures like old boots and sneakers, school posters, bunny pajamas, one lone coonskin cap from Davy Crockett days, a warped hula hoop, and a pair of skates with five wheels.

It was time to have fun with the kids. They could hardly wait for night to come, and neither could I. I had plans for some fun, at their expense.

Let's see, there were Rickey, Audrey Anne, Rhee, Kelly, Joey, and Lisa, my seven-year-old daughter, and her ever-present Pekingese, Chen-Chen. They had all gathered in my yard to go trickin' and treatin'.

Their mothers were there to accompany them. Me? I stayed behind. I had plans for those little goblins upon their return.

They were hardly out of sight when I put my plan to work. I went back inside and proceeded to put catsup all over my face, neck, hair, and white shirt. Next, I took white shoe polish and painted my hands before reaching for a sheet in the hall closet.

All set, I went back outside and shinnied up a tree next to the back door and draped the sheet over me. Laughing aloud in anticipation, I sat perched on that limb and listened to the screeches and sounds of Halloween in the neighborhood.

I hadn't been on my lofty perch long when I heard them approaching. They had scared all the neighbors and were returning home to take stock of their Halloween bags. I was all set to scare their masks off.

They sounded like a bunch of baby chicks as they came closer. I was all set and waiting. I wanted them to get as nearly under my tree as possible before going into my act. The only mother wise to my scheme was Jane Sheppard,

Kelly's mother, and she led the little goblins right up the driveway to a preselected spot under my tree.

At the appointed time I let out a yell that must have been heard miles away, "Aaaagghhhowwweeeeeeeaaaggghhh!"

Well, sir, you've never seen a group of baby chicks and hens scatter faster! They went into the shrubbery, over the shrubbery, into and around the house, and anywhere else their feet would take them. Silver bells, miniature Snickers, sour balls, jawbreakers, suckers, chewing gum, bubble gum, cookies, and pennies covered my driveway like a hail storm.

Skirts were flying and children were crying. Me? I was laughing. That's putting it mildly. I was hysterical, but not for long.

No need to beat around the bush. I just plain fell out of the tree! When I raised up on my limb to flap the sheet, it got caught on a branch, and I tumbled down. I can tell you, when I hit the concrete driveway, I was all alone. Even Jane had vamoosed.

If you think the yell I let out when the kids got back was loud, you should have heard the one forthcoming when I hit the driveway!

My problems were just beginning. When Jane and the other hens decided to check on this ol' rooster, they all thought I was acting. There I lay with what later was confirmed as a broken arm. I finally convinced Jane that I was hurting.

One thing about it: they all agreed that it was the doggonest Halloween prank they had ever seen. I can assure you that you'll never find me up a tree or out on a limb again on a Halloween night. Why? Because, like I said, "Bo Whaley has determined that trick or treating may be hazardous to your health."

Just Ask the Guy in the Next Seat

Only one person can solve all the world's problems, and wherever you sit, he's usually in the chair right next to you.

I read that on the wall of my doctor's office one day, and it set me to thinking about the many times I've been forced to listen to the unsolicited comments of some blowhard in a restaurant, at a ball game, or in a doctor's office.

How many times have you walked into your favorite breakfast spot, newspaper in hand, and selected a seat way back in the back booth, only to be confronted by some character at a nearby table who isn't hungry, can't read, and is "mad as hell with Reagan"?

"Country's in bad shape, ain't it buddy? That damn Reagan's gonna' have us all in the bread line 'fore he's through. But what does he care? He's got that big ranch out in California and a wife who wears $5,000 dresses and buys china like a drunk antique dealer with seven credit cards and her husband's check book. And who the devil ever heard of payin' $250,000 for a set of dishes? I remember when fillin' stations gave dishes away, don't you?" he bellows.

"Yeah, right," you grunt.

"Remember when a man could buy a dang good breakfast for 75 cents? Now look—two eggs, grits, sausage, toast, and coffee, $2.83. It's a doggone shame, I say," he gripes.

"I guess so, friend," you say, turning the page.

"And how 'bout Lebanon, the PLO, the Israelites, the Gaza Strip, an' all that mess? All they know is fightin', they was raised on it. I tell you what I'd do if I was Reagan. I'd get me a bunch of Marines, call Wesley Gore, M.O. Darsey, and Bud Higgins back to active duty and . . ." he rambles on.

"Right," you say with all the enthusiasm of Leonard Bernstein at a Rolling Stones concert, or Mick Jagger at a Bernstein symphony performance.

You finally give up on the newspaper, fold it away, and concentrate on your two over easy, with chatter—unsolicited chatter.

It almost never fails when I go to Athens to see the Dogs play. I climb and climb and climb and finally reach Section

XX, Aisle YY, Row ZZ, Seat 11. One more row up and I'd be dodging birds and airplanes.

I'm still trying to catch my breath when the holder of the ticket for Seat ZZ-12 arrives. Squeezing him into one seat is like trying to stuff a size forty-six into a pair of size thirty-two knickers.

And he's a football expert, a big-mouthed football expert who guzzles vodka and smokes stinky cigars.

"Dogs ain't gonna' do it today," he announces to one and all.

"Why not?" I ask, wishing immediately that I hadn't.

"Simple. 'Cause Dooley ain't usin' his big yard dog right, tha's why," he says authoritatively.

"His big yard dog?"

"Right. Herschel Walker. Dooley jus' ain't makin' the best use of the boy."

"What do you mean?"

"Jus' wait til' the game starts an' I'll show you," he says.

Meanwhile, he finishes off a fifth of vodka, lights up a stale rope, and succeeds in insulting the sweet thing in YY-13 twice.

"I knew thirteen would be an unlucky seat for me this year, Harry," she whimpers to her husband. (But Harry doesn't hear her. He has the cheerleaders zeroed in with his binoculars. You see, Harry's "game" always begins thirty minutes before kickoff.)

The kickoff finally comes, fatso in ZZ-12 goes into his coaching routine, and Harry in YY-14 has isolated the third cheerleader from the left in his lenses.

"See there! Tha's what I'm talkin' 'bout. Dooley's got Herschel runnin' straight ahead. Dumb! Jus' plain doggone dumb!" he yells.

"But he gained eighteen yards," I say in defense of Dooley.

"Don't make no difference. Oughta' run the big dog wide ever' time he ain't a flanker goin' out for a pass," he says.

This continues for the entire first half and everybody hopes for a breather at halftime. Not so!

"O. K., now let me tell you what Dooley oughta' do in the

second half. First, try an onside kick an' then put the big yard dog at quarterback and . . ." he rambled.

YY-13 and 14 got up and left. Everybody within earshot understood why, except the vodka guzzler and rope smoker.

I have the same luck in doctors' offices that I have in restaurants and at ball games. I no sooner sign in and take my seat and start reading a 1959 issue of *Field and Stream* than the guy in the next chair starts in.

"Did I ever tell you about my days in the Peace Corps? Well, I went to South America and . . ."

He can also tell you how to curb inflation, cure the common cold, solve Rubik's cube, stop unemployment, how to tune up a 1965 Mercury, solve the Atlanta traffic problem, and why gold is so high.

If you sit and listen long enough, he'll explain the situation in Lebanon, tell you how to make a million in the stock market, and what caused Carter's defeat—all unsolicited.

Sorry. No Receipt, No Return

One day I am going to wake up to the realization that to really reap the full benefits that could be mine in department stores I must conform to their policies and procedures.

One policy, and an understandable one, is the policy of saving receipts. You can't return a diaper pin unless you have a receipt to show proof of purchase. I have no argument with such a policy.

My problem is that I have never programmed myself to save receipts. Know where my receipts go? In the first trash can past the check-out counter. And I've regretted it so many times.

I had a dear aunt who was an All-American receipt saver. As the administrator of her estate following her death in 1973, one of my duties was to inventory the contents of her three houses in Hancock County.

So help me, she had eleven trunks—big ones—and each was stuffed to the hinges with worn, yellowed papers. Most were receipts.

She saved receipts for such items as knitting needles, salve, thimbles, string, shoes, dentures, corn plasters, eye drops, grits, books, and an occasional blouse or sweater.

She also saved receipts for insurance payments, club dues, and donations to her church and the Red Cross. Had she been there she would have brought home receipts for the Louisiana Purchase and the sale of Manhattan Island. At the Boston Tea Party her final words would have been, "Don't forget to ask for a receipt!"

All this came to mind when I recently attempted to return an item to a local store without one. I should have stayed home.

The young lady at the service desk couldn't have been nicer. "Can I help you, sir?" she asked, smiling.

"Yes, please. I'd like to return this electric can opener."

"Is there something wrong with it?" she inquired, dutifully.

"Nothing major. It won't open a can," I explained.

"All rightie. Would you like another can opener like this one, or would you prefer a refund?"

"Well, I don't want another can opener like this one, that's for sure."

"Why not, sir?"

"Because it won't open a can," I replied.

"Well, we'll be glad to refund your money. May I see your receipt, please?"

"Well, it's like this. You see, it is that I don't have a receipt but . . ."

"Sorry. No receipt, no return," she announced as coldly as an auctioneer in Minnesota. "Store policy."

"You see, I had a receipt but . . ."

"Right, that's what they all say."

"But this can opener doesn't work. What would you like me to do with it?" I asked, knowing I'd made a boo-boo as soon as I said it.

Ever seen a movie in which a German concentration camp guard is featured? You know, arms folded across chest, chin tucked in, eyes squinting, and right forefinger tapping on left bicep? That was my return item clerk.

She was nice about it, though. She uttered not a word, just stood there, staring and tapping. I could almost read her mind.

Does anybody out there need an electric can opener? It's pretty, has all the latest features, a four-foot cord, and the warranty card is still in the box. It's sitting right on my three-legged kitchen table next to my broken toaster and my electric coffee pot that I tried to exchange last year.

Same problem. No receipt.

You Don't Need a Cart for Just a Few Items

I get off to a bad start in supermarkets by never taking a shopping cart from the stack. This probably dates back to my early bachelor days when I reached for one, got one with ruptured wheels that wouldn't go straight on an AA pledge, and nearly demolished the store by knocking down a mountain of apple sauce, hitting the bread rack head-on, and almost sideswiping a senior citizen.

I always say to myself as I eye the carts, "Only gonna' pick up a couple of items. I don't need one." Have you ever tried to "pick up a couple of items" in a supermarket?

Hear me, friends and neighbors. You can hitchhike to Forsyth, take in a movie, have an ice cream cone at Howard Johnson's, hitchhike back to Me-Ma's for country ham, syrup, and biscuits in Allentown and hoof it on back to Dublin before you can negotiate the check-out with a "couple of items" at the supermarket. They just ain't programmed for bachelors and other singles.

You want to put a halt to supermarket shoplifting? Simple as ABC. Just put a guy on a stool near the front door, give him a cigar box, change for a ten, and a sign, "Single Men Only—No Carts Allowed."

And you won't even need to give Green Stamps. All the

poor guy wants is out with his Vienna sausage, saltines, six-pack, and a couple of rolls of Charmin without a lot of hassle.

It is always my avowed intention when entering the supermarket to pick up something like two cans of soup and a loaf of bread. Hah! The road to the check-out is paved with good intentions.

What I usually end up with (sans the cart) is this: six cans of soup (on sale), Cheer, bread, four cans of apple sauce (the store buyer went ape over apple sauce and you run into mountains of it at every turn)—and I don't even like apple sauce—three cans of Vienna sausage, three bananas, two rolls of Charmin, a tube of toothpaste, one can of sliced peaches, a pound of ground beef, two cans of Hungry Jack biscuits, and a package of cheese, my weakness.

And, remember, no cart. I *never* have a cart.

So here I come, all the way from the meat counter in the back, the most distant point in the store from the cash registers.

Please don't ask me why I didn't *start* at the meat counter. If I was smart enough to answer that, I'd be rolling a shopping cart instead of going into my juggling act up aisle five. And here's the way it works:

First, the toothpaste—shirt pocket; Vienna sausage—two cans in right front pocket, one can in left rear pants pocket; cheese—crammed in pants at the waist near the navel area; one loaf of thick-sliced bread, soon destined to become one loaf of thin-sliced bread—under right armpit; (three bananas join the bread); Charmin, two rolls—under left armpit; ground beef goes between the Charmin; six cans of soup, four cans of unwanted apple sauce, and a can of sliced peaches—you're right, stacked like stovewood from my Timex to my Izod alligator.

Aha! You thought I forgot the Cheer, didn't you? No way. Where does it fit in the scheme of things? Right up there, all snuggy like, under my chin.

All set, I begin my advance toward check-out, walking with all the poise and dignity of a lobster with a double hernia and a broken neck. I approach a doctor and his wife but manage to hide behind an apple sauce mountain to avoid explanations.

As I creep past the crackers and cookies on aisle five, I slip up on the saltines and reach for a box. I grasp it but in so doing a restless can of apple sauce, sensing it's not wanted, escapes, drops to the floor and rolls to aisle six. While I'm trying to capture the wayward sauce a discontented can of Beef Chunky defects to aisle three and eight ounces of mild cheddar slides down my left pants leg. An escapee from the juvenile detention home, riding a shopping cart à la Evel Knievel, runs over it.

I finally limp on to the check-out counter and stand there, a member of the walking wounded, while a sweet little lady proceeds to drop her handbag, thereby dumping an assortment on the counter matched only by grandma's sewing machine drawers.

I was all set to unload when I heard the little guy behind me say, "Excuse me, do you mind if I go ahead? I only have two cans of soup and a box of Cheer."

"Be my guest," I said. "You don't even have a cart, do you?"

"Naaa, never use 'em. I just pick up a couple of items at the time," he said. "Try to avoid the hassle."

"Yeah, I know 'bout them hassles," I mumbled as he left and fourteen "thin" slices of bread dropped at my feet.

Part 2

From the Corners of My Mind

There's an almost lost art in this world, but I am doing my dead level best to revive it. It's called "sitting around." When you're sitting around, you don't really do nothing. You just find a nice, quiet, place by a creek or a river and sit there thinking. Like Uncle Remus sang in the classic movie, *Song of the South*, "Everybody Gotta' Have a Laughing Place." I have mine, a nice camphouse on the bank of Turkey Creek in Laurens County, Georgia. It's called Turkey Run Plantation, and while I don't own it I have a better arrangement than if I did. It belongs to a good friend, and thanks to his generosity I have a key. Most of what I write, including this book, originates there on a large patio extending out over the creek with a flowing well making nature music over my left shoulder.

If nothing comes, a fella can always drop his fishing line in the water and wait. If worse comes to worse, he can bait the hook at the risk of being disturbed.

If the fish don't bite, there's always whittling. Of course, whittling is almost extinct, too. My granddaddy was the last in a long line of dedicated whittlers that I remember, and he died in 1944. Sadly, whittling is a lost art.

The advent of television in the early 1950s signaled the death knell of sitting around, but I refuse to completely give it up. Sitting around is really creative loafing, and I work hard at it.

If you don't own or have access to such a place, try any place that is void of such nuisances as juke boxes, rock bands, and a television set tuned to the wrestling channel.

It was while sitting around at Turkey Creek that thoughts of don't-call telephone directories, hospital patients, television commercials, inventions, miniskirts, senior citizens, occupations, and many more came to mind. I just propped my fishing pole up against the camphouse, closed my knife, went inside, and wrote about them—purging "The Corners of My Mind."

Needed: A Don't Call Directory

Now and then I come across a void and make every attempt to remedy it. Like your telephone directory, for example. Have you ever thought what an invaluable aid it is? If you use it.

Do you know anyone who fits this description? She's between sixteen and twenty. She's addicted to the telephone. She lives with a receiver sticking out of her ear, sprawling on the bed, lying on the floor with both feet on the wall above her head, curled up à la shrimp on the sofa, eating one handed and covering an easy chair like a cheap suit when she talks on the telephone. She can, and does, roll her hair, do her algebra, make faces at her little brother, mix a salad, open a Tab, press her blouse, or do her nails while talking on the telephone.

Her head is permanently tilted forty-five degrees left.

And one other thing. She wouldn't look up a number in the telephone directory if there was a chance she'd win the Irish Sweepstakes. Telephone directories are for somebody else. Does she write the number down for future reference after getting it from 411? Not on your life. She'll be right back in an hour dialing the same number: 411.

I'm sure we've all had our share of unusual experiences with the telephone. My friend, Carl Nelson, Jr., related one of the best I've heard lately.

He says his phone kept ringing and he kept telling the caller he had the wrong number. Somewhat exasperated, and fast losing his patience, he finally told the caller in a somewhat less than pleasant tone of voice, "Look! I've told you three times you've got the wrong number!"

"Well, if I'm calling the wrong number, why in the heck do you keep answering?" the caller shouted back.

I guess what really prompted this chapter was a message on my desk one day. It was on one of those little pink slips headed "Telephone Message."

The person receiving the call just fills in the blanks.

Mine was a message that a teacher at a school had called. The appropriate blanks were filled in. "You were called by————." "Left this message————." "Please call him at————."

The time of the call was recorded, 9:25 A.M.

I tried. Honest I did, until 2:15 P.M., when I had to go to an important meeting on Country Club Road. Since there are no pay phones on the tees and greens, I asked our secretary to return the call for me. She tried, until 4:00 P.M. No luck. She heard the same thing I did when she dialed the number. "Bzzz. . . Bzzz . . . Bzzz."

I would like to propose that we create a Don't Call telephone directory. It will save you a lot of time if you'll just tack this on the wall above your telephone.

The Don't Call Directory
Unless you are one of those who just love to sit and listen to repeated "Bzzz . . . Bzzz . . . Bzzz," don't call:

• Any school between the hours of 8:30 A.M. to 3:30 P.M.

• Any household after 3:45 P.M. wherein a teenager resides who is going steady, just broke up with her steady, or has an algebra test in the morning.

• Any household wherein the occupants have recently returned from a winter vacation in the Bahamas, had a dog bite a neighbor's child, or the neighborhood has just been zoned commercial unexpectedly.

• Any household where the woman next door has recently been a guest on the Phil Donahue Show.

• Any household wherein the wife is the chairman of the

neighborhood citizens' committee to secure signatures on a petition to prevent one hundred Dempsey Dumpsters from being put in the neighborhood.

• Any household on Saturday or Sunday night if the guy living there had a hole-in-one in the afternoon.

• Any household on Sunday morning whose house has been "rolled" the night before.

• Any store that advertises ground beef for 59 cents a pound and milk for $1.29 a gallon followed by the announcement Free Delivery.

• Any household where a student arrived home that day after spending Spring Break at Daytona Beach or Panama City.

• Any household that has run an ad in the daily paper: Free tickets to Willie Nelson concert. Have eight and can't go.

You don't believe me? O.K. Go ahead and call. And if you need the number, just dial 411. You meet the nicest ladies that way. One thing for sure, you won't get a busy signal!

What Should They Be Doing for a Living?

It has come to mind recently that many well-known individuals look right in the position they hold, and many do not. I think we have stereotyped what people should look like in designated positions and those that veer from the mold just don't fit.

For example, Ronald Reagan looks like a president; Jimmy Carter does not. Spiro Agnew looked like a vice president, Dan Quayle does not. Carl Sanders looked like a governor; Joe Frank Harris does not. Norman Vincent Peale looks like a preacher; Oral Roberts does not. Get the picture?

There are thousands who look like square pegs in round holes. Today I'm listing just a few, their positions, and based on their appearance what they should be doing for a living.

• *John Madden,* CBS television sportscaster: Automobile salesman at the Tom Stimus madhouse in Forsyth.

• *Zell Miller,* lieutenant governor of the state of Georgia: Salesman at Honest John's Discount Clothing, Calhoun, Georgia.

• *Oprah Winfrey,* TV talk-show hostess: Night waitress at Bobby Joe's Bar-B-Que and Transmission Repair, Talladega, Alabama.

• *Joe Frank Harris,* governor of the state of Georgia: Statue in the Wax Museum, St. Augustine, Florida.

• *Barbara Walters,* TV newsperson: Prop her up next to Joe Frank.

• *Oliver North,* retired USMC lieutenant colonel, among other things: Manager of Ace Loan Co. and Pawn Shop, Phenix City, Alabama.

• *Bella Abzug,* former U.S. congresswoman from New York: Mud wrestler at "Slick" Barton's Mud Wrestling Emporium, Morgantown, West Virginia.

• *Joan Rivers,* deposed TV talk-show hostess: Bella Abzug's opponent at "Slick" Barton's Mud Wrestling Emporium, Morgantown, West Virginia.

• *Ted Kennedy,* U.S. senator from Massachussetts: Stand-in for Kermit the Frog.

• *Dan Quayle,* vice president of the United States: Towel boy at the Rub-A-Dub-Dub Massage Parlor, Nashville, Tennessee.

• *Pat Sajak,* rookie late-night TV talk-show host: Umbrella and raft renter at Malibu Beach, California.

• *Ted Turner,* owner, Turner Broadcasting Co.: Oil rig roughneck, Port Arthur, Texas.

• *Phil Donahue,* daytime talk-show host: Sorry, I can find no place where Donahue fits.

• *Sam Nunn,* U.S. senator from Georgia: Male nurse, Henry Grady Hospital, Atlanta, Georgia.

• *Andrew Young,* mayor of Atlanta: Tour guide at Disneyworld.

• *Herman Talmadge,* former governor of Georgia and U.S. senator: Owner and operator of Herman's General Store, Route 2, Helena, Georgia.

• *Tom Murphy*, speaker of the Georgia House of Representatives: Loan officer for any bank owned by Bert Lance.

• *Conway Twitty*, country music singer: Hairdresser at Wash and Wear Hair Salon, Hendersonville, Tennessee.

• *Roy Acuff*, same as Twitty: Justice of the peace, Pine Bluff, Arkansas.

• *Danny Ford*, football coach, Clemson University: Ferris wheel operator with James H. Drew Shows.

• *Jim Bakker*, impostor: Waiter at Harold and Jarrel's Lovely Lunch, San Francisco.

• *Jimmy Swaggart*, impostor: Fertilizer salesman for Aromas Unlimited, Slidell, Louisiana.

• *Willie Nelson*, singer: Chicken plucker at Herb's Chicken Ranch, Gainesville, Georgia.

• *Whoopi Goldberg*, actress: Pants presser at Nu-Way Cleaners, Waycross, Georgia.

• *David Letterman*, late-late-night TV talk-show host: Rack boy at Charlie's Pool Room, Paducah, Kentucky.

• *Geraldo Rivera*, daytime TV talk-show host: Short order cook at the Grease Pit, Clio, South Carolina.

• *Bob Barker*, TV game show-host: Cosmetics salesman for Pimple & Acne Products, Boise, Idaho.

• *Pat Robertson*, full-time TV Christian broadcaster and part-time presidential candidate: Fuller Brush salesman.

• *Dan Rather*, CBS News anchor: Assistant editor, *Grier's Almanac*.

Mysteries to Ponder While Driving

I have often wondered what people think about while driving for long periods of time alone. I have friends who live on the road. Joe Durant could probably drive to Albany or St. Simons blindfolded. My daughter could make it to Macon easily with both eyes closed. And what about over-the-road truckers? What do all these people think about as they drive?

And what about me? I decided I would find out last week

while making the 275-mile round trip to Columbus via
Georgia 96. I always keep a legal pad on the front seat next
to me and, when I arrived back in Dublin, I had filled five
pages.

Here are some of the things that crossed my mind as I
drove along:

Why don't Mercedes cars have white sidewall tires?

Does anybody drive fifty-five any more?

Why would anybody pick up a hitchhiker?

How many million radio stations are there in Georgia?

What do nudists do with their hands when they're just
standing around talking?

Is there really a difference between crispy and extra-
crispy; or unleaded and superunleaded?

Is the Miss America contest all that important? If so,
then tell me who won in 1985.

Are root canals cheaper in Panama?

Does Alaska have traffic lights? If so, do they say Mush
and Don't mush?

Is a watermelon red on the inside before it's cut open?

Where do the seeds for seedless oranges come from?

Are left-handed people discriminated against?

Do all nurses have cold hands?

Would Benjamin Franklin have played golf in a lightning
storm?

Does anybody know the whereabouts of Herb? Does anybody care?

Do plumbers repair city water tanks? If not, who does?

What the heck is a Plymouth station wagon from Ontario
doing in Bonaire?

Does the San Diego Chicken ever eat at Kentucky Fried
Chicken?

Does Tom Stimus have jumper cables?

Does Dolly Parton inhale more than she exhales?

What do people who man firetowers think about?

Would dog collars work on fleas?

Who among you has ever held a winning raffle ticket? Do
they ever actually hold the drawing?

How many keys do you own that don't fit anything?

Are the Goodwill Games over? If so, who won?

Is Greg Norman a pool shark?

Is it legal to put bumper stickers on the rear window if you have no rear bumper?

Is it possible to read between the lines if the copy is single-spaced?

Do lawyers object at weddings, too?

Is it considered socially acceptable for a policeman to use a nightstick in the daytime?

If a fast-food restaurant gives slow service, could it then be characterized as a half-fast-food restaurant?

Is it possible to offer only medium and large Cokes for sale, but no small ones? Tell me, how can you have a medium without a small and large?

Does the little girl in the Coppertone advertisement ever get sunburned?

Do highway crews in Atlanta open the main highway while they're repairing the detour?

Is there an organization for people who are being driven to drink? Maybe the AAAAA?

During an election year when we're bombarded with political speeches and ads, I always think about the question posed by a small boy to his father after spending an hour walking through a cemetery. "Daddy, where do they bury all the bad people?"

Do farmers get up to watch the Late, Late Show?

Is it true that a small South Georgia town has a guy who drinks so much that he's invited to birthday parties to blow on the candles to light them?

That's one way to spend 275 miles. It won't win a prize, but it will keep you awake. Try it on your next trip.

Words Hospital Patients Don't Want to Hear

You know what a hospital room is. It's where friends of the patient go to talk to other friends of the patient. Never mind that the patient is gagging and turning blue. The visitors are going to discuss such things as the weather, taxes, Reaganomics, the Busbee retirement pension, too much rain or the lack of it, income taxes, and "the time I had my operation."

I'll tell you, Dr. Kildare, here are a few things that, as a patient, you don't want to hear in your hospital room:

- "Well, I don't think he should buy any long playing records."
- "It's a very rare disease. The only other time I've seen it is in a crossword puzzle."
- "I won't tell you where we found the skin to graft on your husband's chin, but occasionally his face may feel like sitting down."
- "We performed that operation just in the nick of time. Another few hours and you would have recovered without it."
- "What? Three thousand dollars for an exploratory operation on my wife? Forget it, I'll find out what's wrong with her at the autopsy."
- "I think my doctor used to be a veterinarian. He just told me to open my mouth and say, 'Moo.'"
- "Yes, we have to operate. My malpractice premium is due tomorrow."
- "Hmmmm, I thought they cured this years ago."
- "Down at the plant, they painted out your name in the parking lot this morning."
- "With this confounded new metric system, I can't figure out this thermometer. Either he has a temperature of 415 degrees or he's going eighty-five kilometers per hour."
- "If you're going to put money on today's football game, I suggest you bet only on the first half."
- "I wouldn't bother watching 'All in the Family' tonight. It's a two parter."
- "Of course I wear a mask when I operate. That way, they're never sure who to blame."

And finally . . .

Doctor: "I can't find the cause of your liver trouble, Henry. But offhand, I'd say it was due to heavy drinking."

Patient: "I understand, Doc. Why don't I just come back when you're sober."

Cathouse Investment Doesn't Make Sense

There are two return addresses that scare the devil out of me: the Internal Revenue Service and any law firm. Last week I found an envelope on my desk with this threat in the upper left hand corner: "Law Offices, Jones, Jones & Hilburn." My initial reaction was to call Judge Towson and plead guilty. My second was to leave town as soon as possible. But I opened it, migrating to the darkest corner of the men's room to do it. You know, lawyer-client relationship and all that jazz.

I had just ripped the envelope open when Daryl Gay, sports reporter at the Dublin *Courier Herald,* walked in on me.

"Hey, Bo! You all right?" Daryl asked.

"Uh . . . yeah, fine," I stammered.

"Then what'cha doin' down on your knees behind the commode with a flashlight and the lights turned off?"

"Oh, nothin'—just opened this secret envelope from Washington," I lied. "Have to open it in the dark because of the secret ink that disappears in the daylight."

"Whatever you say, Bo," the fisherman sighed.

I thought he'd never leave, but he did and I removed the letter from the envelope. It was typed real official like by "vhy" on Jones, Jones, and Hilburn stationery. As I read it I wondered what "vhy" must have thought as she took the dictation and typed it. Probably something like, "Egad! I went to secretarial school for this?!" Here's what I read by the dawn's early flashlight while crouched behind the commode:

Dear Bo:
    I recently read of an investment in *Florida Sportsman Magazine.* Knowing you are an astute investor, I thought maybe you would like to participate with myself and

about two others in this endeavor. A $50,000 investment is required. However, with the following prospectus I do not believe we would have any difficulty in obtaining the investors, as we are getting in on the ground floor.

The business is raising cats. We could start with one million female cats and one tom cat. Each female cat gives birth to an average of twelve kittens per year and catskins can be sold for an average of thirty cents each, producing a gross revenue on twelve million skins of about $3.6 million dollars per year or $12,000 per day, excluding Sundays and holidays.

A good catskinner can skin about 200 cats per day, at a wage of $26 per day. I figure we would need about 200 catskinners, so the profit would be $6,800 per day. Therefore, our initial $50,000 investment can be recovered in 7.35 days. Really, Bo, it beats any investment I ever heard of.

In the beginning, the key to operating successfully is that we will have a rat farm adjacent to the cat farm and will feed the rats to the cats. Since rats multiply four times faster than cats, our stock of four million rats will be enough to feed each cat four rats per day. Conversely, one cat, after being skinned, will feed four rats. In other words, the cats eat the rats, the rats eat the cats—and we get the skins.

Research is very heavy in the area, and we could hope to eventually eliminate the rat farm, as very soon we would be able to cross cats with snakes. The cats could then skin themselves twice a year, which would save the cost of skinning the cats and increase our profits many times over. Until the rat farm is eliminated, however, our wives and/or secretaries would have to help out by working in the rat house. The men can attend to the business in the cathouse.

I'm sure that after considering this you will want to participate in this lucrative farm. Contact me and we will discuss it further.

> Sincerely yours,
> Eric Jones
> ELJ/vhy

You may be interested in my reply.

Dear Eric:

Thank you for your recent letter inquiring of my interest in investing in a cathouse. I bounced the idea off a few friends at Ma Hawkins, and based on their reaction (shock!) I don't feel that I can afford to participate in the venture. You know how that Ma Hawkins crowd is. The news spread like wildfire.

As a matter of fact, I am in deep trouble for even considering the cathouse investment. I have lost my front table seat at Ma Hawkins; been suspended by the Elk and Country clubs; been given the silent treatment by my next-door daughter; declared persona non grata by the National Organization of Women; received a real nasty letter from Garfield and a telephone threat from Mickey Mouse; plus I've been dropped by my golfing partners, Carl Nelson, Jr., Frank Seaton, and Henry Bozeman; and my subscription to *Animal World* has been canceled. My long-time girlfriend, Kitty Litter from Willacoochee, has broken our engagement but kept the ring.

Also, it is rumored that Jackie Beacham and the humane society are considering a court suit against me, along with Jimmy Allgood. Do you know where I might find a good lawyer?

And that's not all, Eric. I was wandering around in the composing room here at *The Courier Herald* this morning and this headline has already been set: Ex-FBI Agent Invests in Cathouse!

I tried to call you on Friday but "vhy" told me you were talking with a client. I did, however, have a long and interesting telephone conversation with "vhy," and I feel it only fair to tell you this. She's leaving you and coming to work for me on July 15.

Sincerely yours,
Bo Whaley

Television Commercials Don't Tell It Like It Is

I'm convinced that the market most in need of revitalization is the TV commercial market. Commercials simply don't tell it like it is. Whatever became of truth in advertising?

A recent commercial advertised a thing called Trim-Trak, a little contraption that resembles a railroad motorcar and slides back and forth on a little piece of railroad track. A long, lean, and lanky girl who looks like Twiggy's sister makes the thing go back and forth by pulling on a handle. The TV pitch is that Trim-Trak will slim a person down and transform the body from the Bella Abzug look to the Twiggy look.

Well, the girl operating the Trim-Trak on television doesn't need it. Heck, she won't weigh ninety-seven pounds soakin' wet! If the TV people want to show it like it is, why don't they put some ol' gal on that thing who's shaped like a Dempsey and has arms like Popeye? And show her huffin', puffin', gruntin', an' sweatin' a lot. The model who demonstrates the Trim-Trak on TV now don't sweat at all. And she ain't even breathin' hard when she stops pumpin'.

Another TV farce shows a fella shampooing his hair, with all the shampoo sittin' on top of his head. That just ain't the way it happens, Selsen Blue. What about the eyes? I ain't believin' the shampoo commercial 'til it shows me a guy who's blind as a bat with shampoo in both eyes desperately trying to feel his way to the towel holder in search of relief and running into the commode and lavatory along the way. And show him stumbling over the trash can and stumping his toe on an open closet door.

I guess the commercial that confuses me more than any other is the one where a guy dressed in a nice clean shirt passes his chewing tobacco around to four or five guys, also wearing nice clean shirts. They all fill their jaw to capacity and immediately become converts to the new chew. But— tell me this—when do they spit? I ain't never seen one of 'em spit. And if you spit enough, the brown juice gets on the front of your shirt.

Let me write the chewing tobacco commercial, and I'll show you a man sitting by the fireplace reading *The Progressive Farmer* or *Grier's Almanac,* pausing periodically to spit over his hound dog and into the fireplace. Tobacco juice will be on his chin and the front of his overalls, with a smattering on the dog.

Of course, everybody is always so nice and agreeable in television commercials. Just once I want to see a guy, in obvious discomfort, walk into a drug store, ask for talcum powder, and have the clerk say to him, "Just walk this way, sir." And then have the customer say, "Hell, lady, if I could walk that way I wouldn't need the talcum powder!"

Just once I'd like to see a Timex watch retrieved from the briney deep at 3:00 P.M. after having been strapped on a submarine propeller for three years, and let John Cameron Swayze remove it only to find that it's deader than the Mondale-Ferraro campaign—and the time 4:22 A.M.

Also, I have no reason to doubt the mechanical qualifications of Mr. Goodwrench. But for goodness sake, smear a little grease on his cheek and one ear and dirty his hands and fingernails up a little bit. Also put a dab or two of used motor oil on the back of his shirt, and maybe one shoulder, as evidence that he crawled underneath at least one car and checked the oil pan, differential, or transmission. Turn off the microphone, but move in close with the camera and capture his expression when the vice-grip pliers slip off a bolt holding the alternator brace, causing him to scrape all the knuckles on his left hand on the fan. And show the anxiety on his face while he tries desperately to replace a stubborn nut way down under in a remote area underneath the power steering unit. Watch him fume as the overheated radiator spews boiling water all over him like Mount Vesuvius at the height of an eruption.

Here are a few other things I'm anxiously waiting to see in TV commercials:

- I want to hear a guy in a beer commercial burp, or excuse himself after a dozen or so to go to the rest room.
- I want to see the dog on the Alpo commercial turn up

his nose at the bowl of dog food and sit there and scratch under his flea collar.

• I want to see the fella promoting powder to make you stop itching scratch now and then.

• I want to see the man advertising Roach Pruf stop in the middle of the commercial long enough to stomp a pair of roaches with the sole of his shoe, the only sure-fire way to get rid of the little devils.

• I want to see the girl who takes the Mazda out for a demonstration ride drive all over Atlanta looking for a parking place like I have to do as opposed to the TV commercial that shows her pulling into a wide open space right in front of the Ritz-Carlton, smack dab in the middle of town at 4:45 P.M., the height of rush hour.

Know something else? I've frequented grocery stores and supermarkets for the past forty-five years and I've yet to see anybody chastised for squeezing a roll of Charmin. And neither can I remember my family ever gathering in the living room to discuss the merits of our toilet tissue.

The Top Ten Inventions Somebody Should Create

Ever get the feeling that all the inventors are on strike? Where are all the modern-day Edisons, Franklins, Bells, and Whitneys when you need 'em?

Think about it for a minute. What has your inventor come up with for you lately? Ball point pens, dacron, polyester, nylon, formica, pop-tops, no-returns, acrylics, flouristan, naugahyde, polyethylene, styrofoam, transistors, micronite filters? Bah, humbug! Let's get the show on the road! Let's face facts. Inventors just ain't gettin' the job done.

Millions, literally millions, of dollars are just waiting to be made with the right invention. If I were an inventor, here are the first ten things I'd invent to become a millionaire:

1. Phone-a-Bath. This would be an adaptor connected to your telephone with a wire running to either your shower or

bathtub nozzle. After two rings, the caller would hear splashing water and a very amateurish voice straining through the chorus of "Singin' in the Rain," thereby signaling the caller that you're taking a bath.

Alligator clips could be used for easily transferring the connection to any other bathroom fixture desired.

Can't you just picture Anita Bryant calling and being greeted with a verse of "Rub-a-Dub-Dub, Three Men in a Tub?"

2. A spray that golf balls could be coated with to make them float. Trav Pollack and I would save a fortune on Number Twelve alone. The way it is now, we have a heck of a time having enough balls to get past Number Three!

3. A litterbag, built into the front floorboard of your car, with no bottom. From the looks of the roads these days, it would save a lot of time. You know, rolling the window down and all!

4. Spray-Sweat. A guy can spray himself and his jogging suit with Spray-Sweat before returning home after having told his wife he was going to run but spent forty-five minutes with the boys having a beer just two blocks from his house. Also, a product that could be called Instant Droop to be sprayed on the socks. What the heck! If you're gonna' lie, go all the way!

5. Golfer's Pal. A solution, sold to men only, that is colorless and odorless and comes complete with a dropper. One drop in the gas tank of your lawn mower guarantees that it won't start for exactly forty-eight hours or, from 8:00 A.M. Saturday until 8:00 A.M. Monday, when you are safely back at work. Use a drop and a half for Labor Day weekend!

6. A noiseless dollar bill changer to be installed on the back of all church pews. (No further explanation necessary.)

7. Cry Baby! A lot of potential in this one. A capsule sort of thing filled with onion juice and secreted inside a rose in the queen's bouquet at all beauty pageants to insure that the winner lets those tears fly when she is supposed to. Can anything be more embarrassing to Miss Willacoochee than to win and then be unable to cry? (Price should be slightly higher in Atlantic City.)

8. Personality Eliminator. This is made of hundreds of tiny transistors and attached to the back of your TV set. It would automatically switch channels when Howard Cosell, Joe Garagiola, Bert Lance, Barbara Walters, Guy Sharpe, or Gail Janus appear on the screen.

9. Rolling Lawyers. This one would take a lot of planning, but it could be very successful. It is a throwback to the old rolling store of the 30s. It could be done by utilizing a Ford Econoline Super Van equipped with a desk and a typewriter. This is the way it would work:

The Rolling Lawyer would follow close behind the rural mail carrier as he deposits all that unsolicited junk mail in the boxes. What is the feature of the Rolling Lawyer plan? Simple: he would be right on the spot to file suit on behalf of the recipient against the sender, and hand carry the legal paper to the mail carrier at the next stop. Can you think of a better slogan for the rolling barrister than, "Sam Smith, Attorney. Specializing in Same-Day Junk Suits. Satisfaction Guaranteed or Double Your Junk Back!"

10. Rent-a-Ring. This should definitely be a money maker! With the divorce rate what it is, and climbing every day, Rent-a-Ring is a natural. It could be merchandised through the same companies that rent formal wear. A wedding ring could be rented by the day, month, or year with the stipulation that, should the marriage last a year, the entire rental amount paid would be applied to the purchase price.

Are You Miniskirt Material?

I have to feel somewhat sorry for today's women and the elevatorlike movement of their hemlines. I mean, they have no way of knowing what's in and what's out as to length. What's a woman to do?

I can see a whole new world of opportunity in the world of miniskirts for some enterprising entrepreneur. It might even rival the American and New York Stock exchanges, and I can just hear some of the girls calling their broker for the early morning Hemline Report. I think it would go like this:

"Good morning! Klein, Vanderbilt, Cassini, California Girl, and Izod. May I help you?"

"Yeah, this here's Robbie Nell Bell, from Alma (Robbie Nail Bail, fum Almer). I'm gittin' ready to go to work at th' facktry over in Douglas an' I need to git th' Hemline Report f'r today. Ya' got it?"

"Yes, Ms. Bell, or is it Bail?"

"All depen's on where ya' fum, Honey. If'n you fum up Nawth, it's Bell; daoun heah it's Bail. Robbie Nail Bail."

"Very good. I'll just go with Bell if that's all right with you."

"Whatevah turns you on, Sugah. Naow then, how 'bout that hemline report? I'm runnin' late, gotta' drop the young'uns off at Mommers, git some gas an' cigarettes, an' have th' left back tire checked."

"Right on, Ms. Bell. Today's Hemline Report shows dresses up 3¼, skirts up 5⅜, and suits down 1⅛. The hemline market is upward and steady, pushing needles and thread to an all-time high according to yesterday's closing quotes. I hope this report has been of some assistance to you."

"Skirts is up 5⅜, eh?"

"Yes, that's correct."

"Great! Mine's right on target so I don't have to fix it this mornin'. Know whut that means, Sugah?"

"Hardly."

"Means I got time ta' stop by Mel's Juke f'r a beer, that's whut! I thank ya' f'r th' information an' all. Y'all come, ya' heah? Bye."

Some time ago a friend gave me a quiz regarding the revived miniskirt craze. About three women in one hundred look great in a miniskirt, and simple math shows that leaves ninety-seven wandering around wondering what went wrong. If you would like to take the quiz, here it is with a little introduction:

If you are recognizably female, start with 15 points. If you score 25 and above, rush out and buy a miniskirt. America needs you walking the streets. If you score under 25, do yourself, and everybody else, a favor and sit this one out. If you want some *real* excitement, take the quiz with a friend, or have your husband or boyfriend take it with you.

THE MINISKIRT APTITUDE TEST

	Me	You
	25	25
Has anyone ever, while you were wearing jeans, looked at you and said, "I bet you'd look great in a miniskirt?" If so, 8 points.	___	___
If your legs are too long to stretch out straight in your bathtub, 10 points.	___	___
Can you put on your tennis shorts, bend sideways in front of a mirror and be happy with what you see? If so, 5 points.	___	___
If on your wedding day people told you you should wear long dresses more often, subtract 2 points.	___	___
If you shave your legs only when you feel like it, subtract 1 point.	___	___
Do your thighs jiggle when you walk? If so, subtract 2 points.	___	___
Are your ankles and your calves the same diameter? 0 points.	___	___
If anyone, anywhere, has ever mistaken you for Tina Turner, give yourself 50 points and stop this foolishness right now.	___	___
Can you pinch an inch on your knee? Subtract 1 point.	___	___

	Me	You
Do you look at the lean and long models in fashion magazines and relate to them as sisters in fashion? 15 points.	—	—
Has your husband ever said he loved you because there's so much to love? Subtract 1 point.	—	—
If your legs are twice as long as your arms, 10 points.	—	—
If your arms are twice as long as your legs, subtract 10 points.	—	—
Can you wrap your index finger and thumb around your ankle? 1 point.	—	—
If you ever avoided buying a bikini for what you called "obvious reasons," subtract 3 points.	—	—
Has the word "toothpick" been used to describe you, or your legs? No points.	—	—
Do you put on high heels and your legs don't look any better? Subtract 1 point.	—	—
Are varicose veins any part of your life? No points.	—	—
Has any male ever confided in you that he thinks you have beautiful legs, but then asks why you have them on upside down? Subtract 5 points.	—	—
If you were a cheerleader in high school and can still fit into your uniform, 8 points.	—	—

	Me	You
Were you once, or are you now, a Rockette? 25 instant points.	___	___
TOTAL:		

If you have any doubts—*any* doubts—about whether you'd look good in a miniskirt, you probably wouldn't. Some things are best left covered. Save your money. Buy a winter coat.

Southern Culture Has a Language All Its Own

Over the past several years I seem to have earned the title, "King of the Rednecks." That's fine with me. Rednecks have been extremely kind to me and I accept the title with a certain degree of humility.

I make no claim of being the ultimate authority on rednecks, but I don't take a back seat to nobody when it comes to southern culture. I've observed and studied it all my life and I'm proud to be a part of it. I also spent fifteen years of my life in the North and came to know some mighty fine folks in places like Detroit and Marquette, Michigan, New Jersey, and New York. But most of all, the absence from Dixie served to broaden my appreciation of, and love for, it.

One of the more noticeable differences between those of us "down here" and those "up there" is the way we talk. Of course, everybody north of the Mason-Dixon Line has the mistaken idea that everybody below it talks like Andy Griffith, and those of us down here picture everybody above it as talking like Archie Bunker.

I won't touch on the northern accent here but will concentrate on some of the words and expressions a Yankee might hear when visiting God's country.

In my book, *The Official Redneck Handbook,* I devoted no less than twelve pages to 110 words that are a part of our everyday language here in the Southland. Today, I'm adding twenty-three more expressions that came to me from my good friend Vicki Allen.

Chances are you have heard these words many times, but for any Yankees in the area who haven't: clip and save for future reference:

Par *(Power):* "Do y'all think 800 horse par is too much f'r a twelve-foot bass boat?"

Achoo *(That you?):* "Hey, Joe! Achoo behin' that stump?"

Strack *(Strike):* "Me'n Joe Boy went aout to Seeumpson's Lake yistiddy an' I got me a strack fust time I thowed aout."

Popatoom *(Pop it to him):* What a fisherman does when he gets a strack.

Minnow *(I'm in a):* "Hurry up, Daryl! I minnow hurry."

Line *(Lying):* "Doyle says he caught a ten-pound bass at Lake Sinclair las' Sat'dy, but I bleeve he's line."

Noon *(New one):* "I still got my ol' reel n' rod, but Buddy got his'sef a noon."

Sunny Beach *(#!&&*#&$*):* What one fisherman might call another who beat him to his favorite bass hole.

Fat *(Fight):* "If'n ya' don' git away fum my fishin' spot, me news gonna' fat."

Hominy *(How many?):* "Hominy fish y'all ketch?" (*Hominy* is also used in reference to weird-looking corn imported from Yankeeland.)

Stern *(Stirring):* "Hey, Jessie! How baout stern up them greeits 'fore they git lumpy."

Skier *(Scare):* "I tell ya', Hoss. That ol' rattler shor give Shorty a skier."

Cumanup *(Coming up):* "Looks like they's a bad cloud a' cumanup, Roy."

Huntin' paints *(Hunting pants):* "I see ya' gotcha' some new huntin' paints, Roscoe. Git 'em fer Cris'mus?"

Big Spenders *(Big suspenders):* "Ya' shore got on some big spenders, Woody. I betcha' ain't worried none 'baout y'r britches fallin' down, are ya?"

Rat *(Right):* Opposite of lef.

Snuff *(That's enough):* "Wail, I'm headin' in, boys. I done got th' limit an' tha's snuff."

Spore *(So poor):* "My ol' boat's 'baout had it. I'd git me 'nother'n if'n I won't spore."

Hone *(Hoeing):* "Nope, can't go fishin' this e'nin, Luke. Old lady says I gotta' finish hone these peas."

Pyonder *(Up yonder):* "Look up, Jim! See all them doves pyonder?"

Yearn *(Yours):* "Mus' be yearn, Wes. T'aint mine."

Summer *(Some are):* "These rabbits ain't all mine, Pete. Summer yearn."

Pier *(Appear):* "Le's move on 'round the cove, Ray. Don't pier to be no bass heah."

Observations of a Confirmed People Watcher

My hobby is people watching. It's inexpensive, and there is never a shortage of subjects. I've been at it for years.

Yogi Berra is credited with having said, "You can observe a lot by just watching," although I doubt seriously that the famed baseballer ever actually made the statement.

As an avid people watcher, I have observed many things down through the years that stuck in my mind. Just for the heck of it, let me share some of them with you:

• The higher a man rises in his company the harder he is to locate by telephone.

• The prettiest woman at the party will have the meanest and ugliest husband.

• The man who does the bank commercials is not the man who makes the loans.

• At any party attended by fifty people, at least thirty-seven of them will stand in the doorway between the kitchen, where the booze is, and the den, where the hors d'oeuvres are.

• No matter how big the room containing the television, a

five-year-old will manage to stand directly between you and the television set.

• Give one kid a blue balloon and the other a red one and the one with the blue one will want the red one and the one with the red one will want the blue one.

• Put three kids in the back seat and they all want to sit by the window.

• A wife will never ask her husband where he's been if he gets home before she does.

• Ask two people the best way to drive to St. Simons and you will leave them arguing.

• The more money a man has the harder it is to get any of it.

• As soon as a politician is elected to office for the first time, he begins whispering and everything he says to anybody is very private.

• Flowers for the one you love, on no special occasion, are the flowers most appreciated.

• Political television ads never show the candidate talking to a rich man, but always to some guy wearing a hard hat in a steel mill, standing knee-deep in a cow lot, or entering or leaving a factory early in the morning. After the election? Another story. He rubs elbows with those who financed him and hobknobs with the affluent.

• No matter what time you go to the mall, all the parking spaces near the mall entrance are taken.

• The best dressed people are conservatively dressed people.

• People who regularly employ the use of profanity are, for the most part, insecure.

• Recently engaged girls will find a way to do everything from wiping their noses to covering their mouths when they yawn with their left hand.

• I have never witnessed an ugly wedding or a pretty divorce.

• Nobody really knows exactly what to do with the toothpick after spearing and eating the little sausage at a cocktail party or wedding reception.

• It has never been determined exactly what one should do with his hands during a physical examination.

• The hospital expression "Hold for observation" had to come into being as the result of some poor soul walking down a hospital hallway wearing one of those despicable tie-in-the-back hospital gowns.

• The man who is the worst shot at a dove shoot will invariably wind up on the best stand.

• No grandparent ever had an ugly grandchild.

How to Know If It's Going to Be a Rotten Day

There are good days and bad days, right? It usually doesn't take long after rising in the morning to get some indication as to what kind of a day you're in for. Not long ago a friend gave me a list of ways you can know if it's going to be a rotten day. I've given it some thought and have come up with some of my own.

• You wake up face down on the pavement.

• You call suicide prevention and they put you on hold.

• You are sitting in church as the collection plate approaches your pew and the smallest bill you have is a twenty.

• You arrive at your office and a "60 Minutes" team is waiting for you in the reception room.

• Your birthday cake collapses from the weight of the candles.

• You want to put on the clothes you wore home from the party and there aren't any.

• Your twin sister forgot your birthday.

• You flip the TV on and they're showing emergency routes out of the city.

• You wake up to discover your waterbed broke—but then you realize you don't have a waterbed.

• Your horn gets stuck and remains stuck as you follow a group of Hell's Angels on the expressway.

• Your wife wakes up feeling amorous and you have a headache.

• Your boss tells you not to bother to take your coat off and your personnel file is on his desk.

- The bird singing outside your window is a buzzard.
- You wake up and your braces are locked together.
- You walk to work and find that your dress is stuck in the back of your pantyhose.
- You call your answering service and they tell you it's none of your business.
- You dial Butterfield 8, and Richard Burton answers.
- Your dentist tells you that your teeth are perfect—but your gums have to come out.
- Your blind date turns out to be your ex-wife.
- Your income tax check bounces.
- You put both contact lenses in the same eye.
- You take your date to the drive-in movie and she wants to watch the movie.
- You peep through a keyhole and see another eyeball.
- Your pet rock snaps at you.
- Your wife says, "Good morning, Bill," and your name is George.
- After seeing a triple x-rated movie, starring Linda Lovelace and John Holmes, you run smack dab into your mother-in-law as you walk out on the sidewalk.
- You order two eggs, one scrambled and one fried, and the cook scrambles the wrong one.
- You get a hole-in-one on Number Six, and you're playing alone.

How to Know If You're Getting Old

Just like there are sure-fire signs that one is beginning a bad day, there are signs that age is rapidly approaching. Here are twenty-five ways you can know if you are getting old.

- Almost everything hurts, and what doesn't hurt, doesn't work.
- The gleam in your eye is from the sun hitting your bi-focals.
- You feel like the morning after the night before, but you didn't go anywhere.

- The only names in your little black book are MD's.
- You get winded playing chess.
- Your children begin to look middle-aged.
- You join a health club and don't go.
- You decide to procrastinate, but never get around to it.
- You know all the answers but nobody asks the questions.
- Your favorite part of the newspaper is, Twenty-Five Years Ago Today.
- You turn out the lights for economic rather than romantic reasons.
- You sit in a rocking chair and can't get it going.
- Your knees buckle but your belt won't.
- You are 17 around the neck, 42 around the waist, and 106 around the golf course.
- After painting the town red, you have to take a long rest before applying the second coat.
- You remember today that yesterday was your anniversary.
- You just can't stand people who are intolerant.
- The best part of your day ends when the alarm clock sounds.
- Your back goes out more often than you do.
- Your pacemaker makes the garage door go up when you watch a pretty girl walk by.
- The little gray-haired lady you help across the street is your wife.
- You have too much room in the house and not enough in the medicine cabinet.
- You sink your teeth into a steak and they stay there.
- You pay more attention to your food than you do the waitress.
- You realize that you're as old as your mouth but a little older than your teeth.

Are You as Organized as You Should Be?

All right, be honest with me now. How organized are you? Answer these questions for me and see how you stack up.

- Can you locate your U.S. Army discharge within a twenty-four-hour period?
- Can you put your hands on your automobile insurance card without undue delay?
- Have you paid last month's cable TV payment?
- Do you always have to pay the penalty on your water bill because you failed to remit by the tenth of the month?
- Is your checking account in balance, or within fifty dollars?
- Do you have coffee, cream, *and* sugar on hand?
- Do you always have to run like the devil for the last 100 yards on Sunday morning to get to Sunday school before the tardy bell rings?
- Do you enter your place of employment at 8:37 A.M. via the back entrance while devouring a Williamson's doughnut and a cup of Huddle House coffee in a vain attempt to avoid detection by an uncompromising and unsympathetic boss who was previously a CIA supervisor.
- Do *all* the socks in the drawer reserved for them match?
- Do you always appear at the laundromat without an ample supply of quarters?
- Do you always arrive at the airport only thirteen minutes before your Delta flight's scheduled departure? (Delta? Sure. Doesn't *everybody* fly Delta?)
- Do your sausage, eggs, grits, toast, and coffee always get done at the same time?
- Do you board MARTA buses with nothing smaller than a twenty?
- Do you always begin your Christmas shopping somewhere around 6:30 P.M. on Christmas Eve?
- Have you made that will that you promised yourself faithfully in 1958 you'd contact your lawyer about "tomorrow"?
- Can you locate the canceled check for $128.57, dated December 14, 1978, needed for proof of payment of your county taxes?
- Have you *ever* filed for your homestead exemption?
- Is the key to your safe deposit box readily available?
- Are all your receipts neatly preserved and filed in one of

those cute little file boxes? Or do you spend most Saturday mornings digging in trash cans and dumpsters?

• Do you throw away your ticket stub immediately after entering Gate G at Atlanta Stadium to see a Braves-Dodgers doubleheader, only to sit there in the top of the second inning with your negligence hanging out while some black-belt karate chopper hovers over you proclaiming for everybody in Section 131 to hear that you are occupying *his* seat?

• Do you habitually show up at the shop to buy that darling little red sweater the morning *after* the sale ended at 9:00 P.M. the night before?

• Do you drop your quarter in the slot early on Wednesday morning, withdraw a newspaper, sit down to your morning coffee and *then* realize that you bought a Tuesday newspaper?

• Do you take a seat at the head table only to have the front of your shirt open up like the Grand Canyon because you neglected, again, to have that missing button in the navel area replaced?

• Do you always arrange to get in the buffet line at just the right spot to ensure that the guy in front of you stabs around in the fried chicken pan and manages to get the last piece of white meat?

• Do you come to the realization that you really are dumb when you reach for the toilet tissue only to grab hold of a cardboard roller?

• Does your magazine subscription expire the very month the final episode of your favorite story that's been running for five months appears—and the magazine is not sold at newsstands locally?

• Does your preacher pay his annual visit to your home the morning after your brother-in-law has returned to Brooklyn, and ring the doorbell while you are cleaning up the guest room he occupied for seven weeks, only to have you greet the preacher at the door while you're holding a *Hustler, Penthouse, Playboy, National Enquirer, Forum* and two empty vodka bottles?

• Do you arrive home at 3:45 A.M. after a night out with the boys and reach for your front door key only to realize that it is resting comfortably on the chest of drawers in the bedroom where you left it?

• Do you stand before a women's club (of which your wife is president) to speak and realize that the notes you have withdrawn from your inside coat pocket and spread on the podium are in reality the point spreads on the Georgia Tech-Georgetown NCAA tournament game in Providence, Rhode Island, or a series of names and numbers: Sally, 286-4492; Rita, 322-8087 (after 10 P.M.); Monica, 404-922-3445 (if a man answers, hang up, or try to sound like a Cuban asking directions to Six Flags)?

If a majority of these apply to you, you're just not organized.

If none of these apply in your case, I envy you.

What Is a Golfer?

What is a golfer? A golfer is a guy who:

• Will ignore his wife, shun his secretary, hang up on his brother, and lie to his boss, but will give undivided attention to his caddy.

• Will tread the muck and mire of creeks and ditches, and wade through briar and snake-infested swamps wearing $75 slacks and $90 shoes, looking for a $1.25 golf ball.

• Will walk across his lawn with grass and weeds two feet high to get to his car and drive to the golf course where he will methodically survey, inspect, and remove every leaf, pine needle, blade of grass, and insect on the green before putting.

• Will leave his lawn mower, boat, motorcycle, automobile, and garden tractor out in the weather for months, but immediately covers his golf clubs at the first hint of rain.

• Will take an hour to get dressed for church on Sunday morning, but can change clothes quicker than Superman and be on the way to the golf course in less than three minutes after returning home.

• Balks like a stubborn mule at the thought of paying $12

to get the heat pump repaired, but won't hesitate to shell out $115 for a new "miracle" driver that guarantees him that he will never slice again (or so the ad in his golf magazine says).

• Will approve a $50,000 loan, sell a house, transfer a deed, write a prescription (or fill one), or write a newspaper column in a matter of a few minutes, but will study, ponder, examine, and argue over a scorecard for the better part of an hour debating "things," "birdies" and "sandys" worth a quarter each.

• Will stand underneath his carport at 12:45 P.M. with Hurricane David blowing his lawn furniture, barbecue grill, and kid's trampoline down the street at more than ninety miles per hour, and with water hubcap-deep in his driveway, and confidently yell to his wife through the kitchen window, "See ya' later, Dot! I don't think it's raining at the golf course."

• Will sit at his desk in the plant all week, surrounded by hundreds of tons of roaring machinery, but refuses to hit his tee shot on Number Three until the loud-mouth bird in the tree on Number Two stops his infernal chirping.

• Can't help his son with his third-grade arithmetic but can stand on the first tee and figure handicaps and strokes with the accuracy of a bank computer.

• Will neglect the battery in his wife's car for months, jump-starting it one hundred times, but will get up in the middle of the night to drive four miles in his pajamas, robe, and slippers to plug in the battery charger to his golf cart.

• Will bump into and knock down little old ladies and children in the supermarket, plod right through a neighbor's freshly planted lawn, and hopscotch across a just-painted porch, but resembles the Great Wallenda as he carefully avoids stepping in his golfing companion's putting line on the green.

• Will sit at his office desk all morning talking golf, then go to the golf course and talk business all afternoon.

• Won't hold his wife's chair, light her cigarette, or open her car door, but never fails to attend the pin when his partner is putting.

• Won't buy his kid an extra Coke at the basketball game, but just let him break eighty for the first time and listen to him yell in the clubhouse, "OK, bartender, set 'em up! Drinks for everybody, on me! And pour yourself one!"

• Couldn't find his cuff links in his bureau drawer with a magnet and a magnifying glass, but can immediately put his hands on every tee, ball marker, and spike wrench in his cart shed.

• Can't plow a straight row in his garden, has no idea where his property line is, and doesn't know a plumb bob from a crowbar, but can read a green and determine the break more accurately than a surveyor.

• Forgets with regularity his anniversary, daughter's birthday, son's graduation, dental appointment, and church committee meetings, but is *always* on time for his 1:00 P.M. tee time on Wednesday, Saturday, and Sunday afternoons.

• Will take the time to repair a green or replace a divot while his front lawn has holes in it that Smokey the Bear could hibernate in.

• Won't take the wife and kids to the beach for the weekend because he can't stand the feel of all that sand, but will go to the golf course three afternoons a week and play in it for the better part of three hours.

• Won't bend over to pick up a sock or a dirty shirt, replace a loose tile, or pick up the garbage can at home because of "that ol' back injury," but will do thirty-six deep knee bends during the course of a round of golf.

• Wouldn't read a good novel or a periodical if you offered to pay him double the minimum wage, but will sit for hours reading and re-reading an article by Bob Toski in *Golf Digest* on "The Absolute Sure Cure for Slicing and Shanking."

• Will lug fifty pounds of golf equipment several miles in 100-plus degree heat in July, but then come home and sit in his air-conditioned den and, while sipping his favorite drink and puffing on a cigarette, yell for his ten-year-old son to bring him an ashtray.

Finally, a word to the wives. Just remember this: when your husband arrives home from the golf course with beggar's lice and sandspurs covering the bottom nine inches of his wet pant legs, that's not really the best time to ask him, "Did you have a good round today, dear?"

Part 3

When Life Imitates Art

Have you noticed? It's the little things in life that cause the most trouble, like when somebody produces a Saturday morning yard sale with all the grandeur of a Wal-Mart bonanza.

How about when we say things that just don't come out right, like "O.K., buddy, if you don't get out of here and leave me alone, I'll find somebody who can." Or, "She's the kind of woman that the more you see less of her, the better you don't like her." Confusing to say the least.

And if you've never seen a group of little old ladies at their weekly luncheon dividing the check and vainly attempting to make it come out even to the penny, you ain't really seen accounting in the raw.

Shouldn't some government agency do something about the hospital gown dilemma? I think it's ridiculous to put a patient in a 350-dollar a day hospital room and then issue him a 39-cent nightgown. A contortionist couldn't secure it in the back where the ties are, and if you ever have occasion to stretch out belly up on an x-ray table that has been in cold storage for three weeks while wearing one, you will then and there know the true meaning of ICU and Hold For Observation.

Another thing: the electrical engineers keep trying to improve on the telephone and have come out with a cordless remote. A fella could go bananas trying to hook up one to use it.

I can't for the life of me understand why we just don't
leave well enough alone and put a screeching halt to the
things in life that imitate art.

I would much prefer to see the researchers devote more
time to finding a cure for Foot-in-Mouth disease, with
which I am afflicted.

And tell us the truth: Was the moon shot for real, or was
the whole thing filmed on top of Stone Mountain?

Yard Sales Are Growing Faster than Kudzu or the Baptists

I was on the road during a recent weekend and purposely
stayed off interstates, preferring to drive on state roads that
take me through small towns such as Bonaire, Mizell, Junction City, Kingsboro, and Hamilton. I much prefer to see
lazy dogs lying in front yards and children playing and running and getting dirty than to sit under the hypnotic spell of
the center line on interstates. I don't see America on the
interstates, but I do in the hamlets of the land.

If we would only stop now and then and look around us,
we'd find that the American scene is constantly changing.
Remember thirty years ago what would have flashed
through your mind if you had seen piles of old clothes, broken furniture, obsolete household appliances, pictures with
broken frames and a bicycle or two with warped wheels and
flat tires littering a front yard? Sure, somebody was either
moving in or out or had been evicted. Not today. Not in the
eighties! What you would be witnessing would be a yard
sale.

I grew up in small towns in South Georgia, firmly convinced that Georgia would one day be taken over by kudzu
and Baptists. Well, I've changed my mind, friend. I am now
convinced that yard sales will win out.

In a recent Friday edition of *The Courier Herald,* there
were eleven yard sales advertised. (And these are just the
ones that are advertised!)

So, on a recent trip, I started counting the yard sale signs when I was near Fort Valley and for the next twelve miles I counted sixteen. (This is over one per mile, and I only saw one Baptist church and very little kudzu. No doubt about it, the yard sale has taken over!)

Yard sales tend to fall into several different categories. I am going to take a look at three.

The Yard Sale for Charity

This is a good chance for the ladies to get together and dispose of all that junk that has been piling up for years, or decades, in the dusty environs of storage rooms, under the house, or in the attic. It provides a sort of party atmosphere. (And it makes no difference to them if a husband's favorite putter, spinning reel, bedroom shoes or prized collection of past issues of the *Saturday Evening Post* happens to wind up on a three-legged table that he never repaired after promising to do so for fourteen years.)

The Neighborhood Yard Sale

I guess this has to be my favorite. You know as well as I do how they begin. Gloria calls Gail one Saturday morning just to catch up on the news. During the briefing session one or the other asks the question that lights the fuse to the yard sale.

"Whatcha' doin' this mornin'?"

"Oh, you wouldn't believe it. I'm *finally* cleaning out the storage house and getting rid of all that junk."

"Oh? Whatcha' gonna' do with it?"

"I don't know. Throw it away, I guess. None of it's any good."

"Whatcha' got?" (This is the question that struck the match.)

"You know, all the kids' old toys, the old dresser, and all that junk I bought at that yard sale we went to last year!" (This was the answer that lit the fuse.)

Silence prevailed while the fuse burned, and then it came:

"I know what! Why don't *we* have a yard sale!!?"

You know what happened from that point on. The girls piled all their collective junk into a heap on the front lawn, borrowed a piece of Donna's poster paper and a black Crayola crayon, and came up with the sign. They even "borrowed" a telephone pole to nail it on with the only tool poor ol' Mike had left in his tool box, a hammer:

NEIGHBORHOOD YARD SALE
Furniture and Clothing
9 A.M.—Saturday

As it turns out, Gloria bought $37.45 worth of Gail's junk and Gail bought $36.20 worth of Gloria's junk. Not a total loss though. They can each put their purchases out again next year for their second annual yard sale.

And poor ol' Mike? Well, he sort of wandered in after the sale was over and asked a logical question that any husband might ask.

"Anybody seen my putter?" That was the question that set off the explosion!

The Perpetual Yard Sale

Perpetual? Yep, that's right! *Perpetual.* Webster defines the word as "continuing forever."

There is a certain yard on a corner here in Dublin that I drive by every day. From Monday to Friday it is as bare as Kojak's noggin. But come Saturday morning? It looks like the drop area of Bundles For Britain! And the sign is always there, nailed on the telephone pole: Yard Sale Today.

Heck, they are more regular than Haley's M.O. It isn't really a yard sale. It is an unlicensed outdoor retail store with more items for sale than a lot of stores. Nothing wrong with that, though. (I called city hall and was told that a person can have as many yard sales as they like as long as they stay on private property. No license necessary and, presumably, no sales tax, either.)

Every weekend I drive by and expect to see a neon sign glaring and blinking: Yard Sale Today.

The perpetual yard sale? Somehow, it just doesn't seem fair to the legitimate businessman. And where does all the junk come from for the sale every week? I have an idea.

I think there is an outfit up in Hoboken, New Jersey, that manufactures the stuff and ships it out every Tuesday to yard sales all over America. Can you just imagine this telephone conversation?

"Hello, Angelo? This is ol' Buck in Dublin. What happened to my yard sale shipment this week? I really need them broken rockers and picture frames!"

"Sorry, Buck, but we are havin' trouble fillin' orders! Seems like everybody wants the same thing. I put on another shift just to keep up with the rundown shoe orders. Also been havin' a big run on broken dishes and fruit jars. I'll get yours out as soon as I can."

"Shore would appreciate it, Angelo. Think you could double my order on broken bicycles and scooters?"

"No way, Buck! The White House is takin' all I can make!"

"How about old gasoline cans?"

"There's another preferred item. The independent truckers buy all I can produce."

"Well, do what you can for me, Angelo. In the meantime, I guess I'll just have to keep breakin' legs on new tables and shorting out the toasters and electric shavers!"

Foot-in-Mouth Disease Strikes Anywhere

All my life I have been privileged to enjoy good health. Other than the normal childhood diseases like whooping cough, measles, mumps, and chicken pox, I haven't had any health problems. Well, one, a totally unexpected heart situation a year ago.

There is one other malady I should mention—"foot-in-mouth" disease. I've had a chronic case of it for years. Another name for it is "famous last words."

Take a look at some prime examples. Who knows? You may even be familiar with some of them.

• "Don't sweat it, Lois. When the needle is on 'Empty' there is still enough gasoline in the tank to go fifteen or twenty miles." (George to his wife, Lois, two minutes before George started walking I-16 in search of a gas station.)

- "There is absolutely no need to be concerned. My scouts tell me there are no Indians within sixty miles of here." (Gen. George Custer to his staff the night of June 24, 1876, during a briefing on the banks of the Little Bighorn River.)
- "I can assure you that everything in my department is as clean as a hound's tooth." (State Labor Commissioner Sam Caldwell to Attorney General Michael Bowers the day before FBI agents arrived at his office to initiate a federal investigation of the labor department and Sam Caldwell.)
- "Nah, state troopers don't patrol county and state roads any more, just the Interstates." (Fred to Jack some eight minutes before being stopped by a state trooper on State Road 338 and ticketed for doing seventy-eight in a fifty-five miles per hour zone.)
- "No, it's not loaded. That ol' shotgun's been standin' in that corner since my grandpa died in 1962." (Ed to his neighbor, Ben, just before blowing the picture of grandpa through the wall of the den with an "unloaded" 12-gauge shotgun.)
- "It won't hurt a bit, Robert. Not with this new high speed drill. You probably won't feel a thing." (Dr. Fraley, dentist, to Robert just before hitting a nerve and watching Robert shoot out of the chair and grab the chandelier.)
- "Nope, he don't bite. Gentle as a lamb." (Uncle Jack to an insurance agent just before he tried to pat Thor, Uncle Jack's bulldog, on the head and thereafter being transported in Uncle Jack's pickup to the emergency room for stitches and a rabies shot.)
- "Well, Homer, I thought it would take at least three days for the check to reach our bank in Willacoochee from Knoxville." (Charlotte to husband, Homer, the day after she wrote a check for two hundred dollars to pay the motel bill at the World's Fair and being notified that the check had been returned, air mail, for insufficient funds.)
- "I'm just glad that my Mary Lou is going to wait until she finishes college to marry Jimmy." (Mary Lou's mama to her friend Louise at Mary Lou's graduation, two days before Mary Lou eloped with Jimmy and married him in Kingsland.)

• "Well, I'll tell you, son. I've smoked four packs of cigarettes a day for forty-three years and it ain't hurt me none."
(Grady B. Wilkins, sixty-three, to a Heart Fund volunteer
on Wednesday afternoon prior to being admitted to ICU on
Saturday night after suffering a massive heart attack.)

• "What? A map? What the heck do I need a map for? I
know the area around Hinesville like I know the back of my
hand. Besides, I'm gonna' take a shortcut through Fort
Stewart." (Wilbur, to his wife, Gertrude, the morning before
the Liberty County Civil Defense Rescue Squad began the
all-night search for them.)

Dividing the Lunch Check by Four Means Confusion

When a fella eats out a thousand times a year, nothing that
happens in a restaurant is surprising.

I thought I'd seen it all the day I watched my Michigan
friend, Nancy Gearhart, trying to eat hushpuppies with a
knife and fork. Not so. That was topped last month as I
dined on barbecued ribs in a restaurant near Lenox Square
in Atlanta.

The hostess seated me next to a table occupied by four
women who had been shopping at Lenox Square.

Shortly after ordering, I heard the beginning of what
would develop into a complicated conversation when their
check arrived. It went something like this:

I can't help it, Ethel; they don't give separate checks
here, and calling it an exclusive dump won't help . . .
What's that, Lois? . . . Ask the waiter again? All right.
Waiter! Yoo-hoo, Number seventeen! Antonio! Sev-unn-
tee-un! Could you come back here, please? . . . Thank you,
Antonio. Could you please go back and make out separate
checks for us?

. . . Oh, I see. You haven't the slightest idea who had
what. You say we changed our minds so many times that

you got confused? . . . What's that, Anne? Howard
Johnson's the next time? Now look, Anne, that doesn't help
us not one whit right now and . . . What? . . . I have no idea
what a whit is, Lois. What's that, Ethel? . . . Split it down
the middle? But that only gives us two checks . . . In quarters? Beg pardon, Lois? . . . Right, I know you're on a diet
and didn't eat as much as we did, but you had the lobster
sauté and that's more than the broiled trout . . . What's that,
Anne? . . . You say Lois had an extra dessert? Well, I don't
think it was extra. It just cost extra because of the whipped
cream.

What's that, Antonio? . . . Just be patient and we'll figure
it out. You're a waiter, so wait. Very well, girls, let's start
over. And you help us, Antonio. O.K., Lois had the onion
soup, the lobster sauté, hold the fries, June peas. What,
Lois? . . . You say you had no June peas? Well, Antonio
says you had them. Anyway, they're free, they come with
the lobster. How much is all that, Antonio? . . . What's
that, Antonio? You say she had a chocolate fudge sundae
with extra walnuts? Hah! Some diet, Lois. All right, so you
didn't have the regular dinner. It was à la carte. So that's
what, Antonio? . . . Seven dollars even. O.K.

Now then, Ethel had the special, corned beef, cabbage,
rolls, tomato juice, and mince pie. Right, Antonio?
. . . What's that? . . . Yes, Ethel is the one with the glasses
and the feathers—in her hat . . . Well, I wouldn't call her
the chubby one, Antonio, but you're entitled to your opin-
ion. Although such a statement certainly won't help your
cause any. So how much is Ethel's special, Antonio?
. . . $5.75. O.K., wait a minute, I have to write this down.
What's that, Ethel? . . . Well, what about the mince pie?
You gave it to Anne because it came with the dinner. But
Anne says she gave you her butterscotch pudding. Which is
worth more, Antonio? Antonio, you are not listening
. . . What's that? . . . You say you have a headache? Well, if
you think you have a headache, what about me?

Wait a minute, what's this for, Ethel? Thirty-five cents
toward the tip? Wait, Anne . . . all right, you can make
change for your tip later. Right now, let's get on with the
check. Hmmmm, Anne had a dessert worth twenty-five

cents more than Lois's. I don't see how it could be worth
more when both came with the dinner . . . Oh, I see it now.
One dinner was worth more.

Ethel, Lois, please don't get the change mixed up. We'll
work out a ratio for the tip later. Isn't that the best way,
waiter? . . . What? You couldn't care less? Well, I don't
consider that cooperation at all.

Now, Anne had the regular dinner: two pork chops,
mashed potatoes, broccoli, onion soup, and all that
. . . What was that, Antonio? . . . Oh, the onion soup is
$1.75? But she had it on the dinner. Anne, I beg you, don't
flare up. Everything will be straightened out. God! This is
worse than the United Nations trying to admit another
country. What, Antonio? Much worse?

You see, Anne, dear, it says, "Choice of soup or ap-
petizer." Not both. Can't you make a small concession here,
Antonio? It might get confusing otherwise. Most places, my
friends claim, give you both on the regular dinner.

What's that, Antonio? . . . I know you have other cus-
tomers. But, for your information, young man, I have to
decide today whether to buy a pair of the most beautiful
shoes you ever laid eyes on, and they're on sale at Rich's at
50 percent off. And pantyhose are a steal at three pair for
$1.85.

O.K., let's add this up. Let's see, two and two is four,
eight and eight is fifteen and one to carry, two, nineteen . . .
hmmm, I get $19.55. . . You don't get that, Antonio? I prob-
ably added it up wrong. . . . Yes, I know there was an extra
coffee. I don't know who had the extra coffee. You don't
charge for extra coffee, do you? . . . Well, most places . . . I
know you don't get coffee for nothing, Antonio. But there is
a vast surplus of the stuff in Brazil. I just read that last
week.

Now, Antonio, shall we be calm and mature about this
and go over it once more just to be sure? Anne had the
lobster sauté which is worth . . . Antonio! Don't tear it up,
Antonio! You don't need to . . .

Well, wasn't that nice of him. He just tore up the check
and said forget it . . . What, dear? . . . Oh, I didn't think he
was screaming as he ran off. I thought he was singing

. . . What is it, Lois? . . . A tip? Yes, of course. He certainly deserves a tip. Let's figure it out. Anne had the regular dinner plus $1.75 for the extra soup . . . What's that, Anne? You won't tip on the extra soup? But at 15 percent it's only twenty-three cents.

I'll tell you what. Next week let's come on Tuesday. According to the menu they have a shopper's special for $2.75, and let's ask for Antonio. He'll like that, don't you think?

Snake under Cabinet Leads to Action, and Traction

I was talking to my WMLT sidekick Bucky Tarpley a few weeks back about favorite stories. I told him some of mine, and he countered with his favorite, an old one but one I still enjoy hearing.

Bucky's Favorite

It seems that a minister was making his appointed rounds at the hospital one morning when he learned that one of his congregation had been admitted late the night before. Naturally, he paid the member of his flock a visit.

Upon entering his room, he saw that the man's right leg was in a cast attached to a traction rig. He also observed a huge knot on his head.

"Well, what in the world happened to you, Wilbur?" the minister asked.

"It's a long story, Preacher, but I'll tell you about it if you'd like," Wilbur said.

"By all means, I'd like to know," his minister replied.

"Well, it all started around midnight. My wife woke me up and said she thought she heard a noise downstairs. She was afraid and asked me to go downstairs and take a look.

"I got out of bed, not bothering to put on my robe, and crept downstairs in my nightshirt. It's old fashioned, I know, but I always sleep in a nightshirt.

"Well, when I was looking around in the dining room

where my wife keeps her silver and china I thought I heard a noise in the kitchen, so I went in there to check and I was standing right next to the refrigerator when I heard the noise again. It appeared to be coming from underneath the sink.

"I slowly removed a flashlight from a kitchen cabinet and tiptoed over to the sink where I slowly opened the door to the compartment underneath, and I heard the noise again. It was a sort of hissing sound.

"I knelt down, switched the flashlight on, and proceeded to look underneath the sink. My head and shoulders were inside the cabinet, and the rest of me was outside. Also, my nightshirt had crawled up to my waist.

"I flashed the light around underneath the sink and soon spotted a snake coiled up in one corner of the cabinet under the drain pipe.

"Well, I considered how I might catch the snake and decided to use a pair of ice tongs that I'd seen on the kitchen counter when I reached for the flashlight.

"I had no earthly idea that my wife's poodle, Fifi, was in the kitchen and just as I eased the tongs out to snare the snake Fifi touched the back of my thigh with her cold nose. Convinced beyond any doubt that I was snake bit, I raised up abruptly, dropped the tongs, and hit my head on the bottom of the sink, knocking myself out," Wilbur told his preacher.

"Well, that explains the knot on your head, Wilbur, but what about your broken leg? How did that happen?" asked the puzzled preacher of his parishioner.

"Well, my wife heard the noise when my head hit the bottom of the sink and, coupled with the frantic barking of Fifi, she came downstairs to see what was going on. She found me unconscious on the kitchen floor and immediately called an ambulance," Wilbur explained. "She told me this morning that she thought a burglar had hit me on the head, knocking me out and running away."

"But I still don't understand what happened to your leg," the preacher persisted.

"O.K., after the ambulance arrived, the two attendants lifted me up and placed me on a stretcher. I regained consciousness just as they started to take me down the back steps.

"One of the attendants, the one holding the foot of the stretcher, asked me what happened and when I told him about the snake and Fifi, he went into hysterics, dropped his end of the stretcher, and I rolled down the steps and broke my leg," Wilbur explained.

Helpful Travel Tips Brochures Don't Print

I travel by automobile a lot and have decided to share some thoughts that might make your travel easier, safer, and more enjoyable. Listed are some of the hazards of road travel that I try to avoid:

- I never pick up two kinds of hitchikers: male or female.
- I make every effort to avoid eating in any establishment that has a jukebox.
- I'm always leery of stopping for lunch at any restaurant that has its specialties misspelled on the sign. Like, "World's Best Cattfish And Hushpupies."
- I watch out for front door signs that say, "No Shoes. No Shirt. No Service." That tells me something.
- I make it a point not to buy gasoline at any establishment that only provides a restroom for its employees.
- I also don't buy gasoline at any place that has a sign on the pump saying, "Pay Before Pumping Gas."
- I pass up any motel that has its night desk clerk imprisoned in a heavy wire cage so that I have to stand outside in the cold and/or rain to register, and then slip my credit card and registration underneath a bullet-proof glass partition like it was visiting day at the state prison, a definite clue as to the kind of neighborhood you're about to go night-night in.
- I shun motels with gift shops that display more playing cards and dice than T-shirts.
- I drive right on by any motel south of West Palm Beach

whose sign says, "Welcome, Señor! Interpreter on Duty 24 Hours a Day."

• I don't consider stopping at any motel whose lounge is twice as large as its coffee shop and dining room combined.

• I never make any attempt to race on the interstates with any car featuring raised white-letter tires bigger than a ferris wheel, obscene bumper stickers, one-way smoked glass, mag wheels, and with fuzzy dice, a graduation tassel, or baby shoes hanging on the rear-view mirror.

• I make it a practice never to shoot a bird at any driver of a high-rise pickup with KC lights on top of the cab, a 30.06 rifle and a .12-gauge shotgun hanging in the rear window gun rack, who's wearing a beard, a CAT diesel cap, and tossing beer cans out the window.

• I never argue with the driver of an eighteen-wheeler, or Mike Tyson, Arnold Schwarzenegger, or Rambo.

• I never check into any motel where the beer cans outnumber the automobiles in its parking area.

• I avoid all motels that require a key deposit.

• I scratch any motel that has a sign in the lobby saying "No Loitering" and/or "Not Responsible for Stolen Property or Broken Car Windows."

• I blackball any motel whose honeymoon suite is the back seat of a 1965 Plymouth parked in the rear, way back by the dumpster.

• I routinely do an about face when I walk in the lobby of any motel where the manager is overhauling a transmission on the floor or cleaning fish on the desk.

• I refuse to register in any motel where the desk clerk is twelve years old or under, unless I'm traveling in Mississippi and she's wearing a wedding ring.

• I mark off any motel that only makes reservations by the hour.

• I make a U-turn at any motel upon determining that to get inside the office and register I'd have to walk around or step over hound dogs, younguns, or tricycles.

• I never check in any motel where the cover charge to get in the lounge is more than the cost of the room.

• I avoid with regularity motels at which more police cars are parked than paying guests'.

Country Boys in the Big City

There must be thousands of stories about country boys going to the big city. I heard two of them while having dinner (supper) with friends in Atlanta.

A young man migrated from the Tennessee mountains down to Atlanta for the weekend. After visiting Grant Park Zoo, the Cyclorama, Stone Mountain, and Six Flags on Saturday, he stopped in at a Cheshire Bridge Road nightspot late that night for a beer.

He hadn't been at the bar more than three minutes when a slinky young girl wearing skin-tight jeans, a low-cut blouse he could read through, spiked heels, and enough makeup to make Tammy Faye look like an Amish wife by comparison, slid onto the stool beside him.

"Hi! I'm Sheila, and I'll do anything you want for two hundred dollars," she said.

"Ya' will?"

"I sure will, Sugah, *anything!*"

He reached for his billfold, removed four fifty-dollar bills, and placed them on the bar.

"O.K., what would you like me to do for you?"

"Paint my house!"

Dove season is here and I'm sure that prompted this one about a South Georgia boy and his new bride.

They were married in June and lived in a small bungalow. He worked hard from sunup to sundown on his two hundred-acre farm. She cooked, cleaned house, and sewed, just waiting for dusk when she would drive his truck to the field and pick him up.

In August, the young husband went to see a doctor in Savannah because his weight had dropped from 190 to 122 during the two-month marriage.

After a thorough examination the doctor told him he was simply exhausted, but he couldn't explain why because he knew him to be an extremely hard worker.

"Do you walk a lot?" the doctor asked.

"Well, yeah, 'bout twenty miles a day, I reckon.

"You walk twenty miles every day?"

"Right, on top o' plowin' all day."

The doctor asked him to explain that.

"Well, it's like this," he began. "Ya' know me'n Bobbie Jean got married in June an'—"

"Yes, I know. I was at the wedding."

"Right, I 'member now. Well, Doc, I jus' love that li'l ol' girl so much that ever' day when I'm in th' field a' plowin' I can't get 'er off'n my mind. So, 'bout twice't in th' mornin' time an' twice't in the evenin' time I jus' drop th' plowline, tie up the mule, an' walk th' two-and-half miles back to th' house, an' two-and-a-half-miles back to th' field jus' to be with her f'r a li'l while, if'n ya' know whut I mean."

"Oh, yes! I know exactly what you mean. I'm not *that* old!"

"Yessir. Well, jus' as soon's she drops me off at the field ever' mornin' an' heads back to th' house, I start thinkin' an'—"

"Hold it! She takes you to the field?"

"Right, early ever' mornin' in my pickup."

The doctor considered what he'd heard for a few moments and then his eyes lit up.

"I have a suggestion. Do you have a shotgun?"

"Yessir. Matter o' fact, I got two."

"Good. Now then, here's what you do. Take one of your shotguns to the field with you every morning and when you feel a strong urge to see Bobbie Jean just fire the shotgun three times as a signal to her that you want her to come to you. Then she can get in the pickup, drive to wherever you are, and after your rendezvous, she can drive back to the house. That way no walking is involved. Understand?"

"Right! Sounds good to me, Doc!"

"All right, but be sure and explain to Bobbie Jean that when she hears the shots she is to drop whatever she's doing, get in the pickup, and drive straight to wherever the shots came from. Have you got that?"

"Oh, yeah! I got it. And thanks, Doc!"

That was in late August. The doctor didn't see him again until they met at a Thanksgiving dinner.

"Well, you look fit as a fiddle," the doctor said. "How much do you weigh now?"

"Back up to 190," the boy replied, sadly.

"Good! And tell me how's Bobbie Jean?"

"I don't rightly know, Doc, I ain't seen her since dove season opened."

Semiprivate Hospital Gowns and Other One-liners

I guess the most famous of the one-liner comedians on the scene today is Henny Youngman. I had the pleasure of a chance meeting and having coffee with Mr. Youngman in the lobby of the Hyatt Regency Hotel in Atlanta a few years back, a most entertaining experience.

You remember Youngman's most famous one-liner, don't you? "Now, take my wife—please!"

And this one: "I was driving my new compact car on Forty-second Street at Broadway and really got into trouble when I put my hand out to signal for a left turn and ruptured a policeman."

Here are some one-liners that just go to show that it really isn't necessary for one to be wordy to get a message across.

• Card playing can be expensive, like any other game in which you hold hands.

• Most of us would be satisfied with enough if the neighbors didn't have more.

• The semiprivate room at the hospital didn't get me down; the thing that really got me down was the semiprivate gown.

• Probably a man's most profitable words are those spent praising his wife.

• Worse than a quitter is the fellow who finishes things he never should have started.

• God took only six days to create the world—but that was before labor unions.

• It's a sure sign the front yard needs picking up when passersby ask if you're having a yard sale.

• The reason many of us can't always recognize opportunity is that it often looks too much like plain hard work.

• When a man brings his wife flowers for no reason—there's a reason.

• Social Security is the guarantee that you'll be able to eat steak when you no longer have teeth.

• If you insist that you can read me like a book, please skip some pages.

• Anybody who doesn't slow down at the sight of a police car is probably parked.

• I finally found a house I can afford, but the only drawback is the dog won't move out.

• Always keep an emergency candle on hand so when the lights go out you can find the toys that have the batteries that were borrowed from the flashlight last Christmas.

• The age of puberty is when your son quits asking where he came from and refuses to tell you where he's going.

• I think this one was written especially for me: A keychain is a device that permits you to lose several keys at the same time.

• For most kids, an unbreakable toy is something used to smash those that aren't.

• There has never been a winter on which you couldn't lay a bet and prove by anybody older that those we used to have were colder.

• Conclusions are an important part of any speech, especially when they come as close as possible to the beginning.

• If there were any justice in the world we would be permitted to fly over pigeons occasionally.

• Nostalgia is thinking about the hamburger that only cost a nickel, but a good memory is what reminds you that it took four to fill you up—and you could afford but one.

• It is good to remember that the tea kettle, although up to its neck in hot water, continues to sing.

• A bachelor is a cagey fellow who has a lot of fun, sizes all the cuties up and never Mrs. one.

• An optimist is a person who thinks a fly buzzing around the house is trying to find a way out without bothering anyone.

• A honeymoon is the vacation a man takes just before he begins working for a new boss.

• What with the rate changes that are occurring, anyone nostalgic for the "good old days" is yearning for last week.

• Never insult an alligator until you have safely crossed the river.

• Good government is like one's stomach; when operating properly, one never knows he has it.

• Inflation has reached the point where we all have to run just to stay in place.

• The beauty of the old-fashioned blacksmith was that when you brought your horse to him to be shod he didn't come up with forty other things that had to be done.

• All of us are smart at ages five and eighteen—at five we know all the questions and at eighteen we know all the answers.

• Children do not seem so taxing when we recall they are deductible.

• Economists are finding out that getting the economy straightened out is about as easy as putting socks on an octopus.

• Paying alimony is like feeding quarters into an empty slot machine.

• Grandparents and grandchildren understand each other because they know how to outwit the middle generation.

Even a Wedding Shouldn't Interfere with Saturday Golf

I like April because it ushers in warm weather and golf, and golf is one of my favorite diversions. I don't play very well but nobody enjoys the fellowship and fun of a foursome more than I do.

I realize that people drive hundreds of miles in spring and summer to splash around in the water and tread in white sand. Heck, I do that on the golf course all the time. There's water on holes three, eight, and twelve at the Dublin Country Club, sand at every turn, and more of the same at River-view. I pass up very few opportunities to baptize a new Titleist on the water holes or bury one in the many sand traps.

Today, specifically, I want to write about a golf tourna-ment that was staged at the Dublin Country Club by (my) teaching golf professional, Joe Durant.

Tagged "The Last Annual Ruthie and Bob Invitational Golf Tournament," the tournament was scheduled for the wedding party in conjunction with the wedding of Joe's daughter to a bogie-buster from Atlanta. The tournament chairman? Joe Durant, father of the bride, who else? No way was he going to let a little thing like his daughter's wed-ding interfere with his Saturday round of golf.

Here are Joe's "Rules Governing Play." I plan to submit them some day to the PGA for incorporation on the pro tour.

1. USGA rules will govern play except where modified by local rules. In the likely event that USGA rules fail to settle disputes, *Roberts Rules of Order* will apply, the tour-nament chairman presiding. Should *Roberts Rules of Order* fail to settle a dispute, then the Queensberry *Rules of Box-ing* will apply, refereed by the tournament chairman.

2. Only white balls will be allowed. This tournament will not be played in technicolor. Fluorescent orange is disgust-ing at nine o'clock in the morning.

3. A ball in your own fairway may be moved a "reason-able(?)" distance without penalty. Any "undetected" move-ment of the ball outside your own fairway will, of course, have to be permitted. I mean, after all, the tournament chairman cannot be *everywhere* at one time.

4. The cow pasture over the fence to the left of Number Five—out of bounds. (Players will please check, wipe, and scrape their shoes, if necessary, before reseating them-selves in the golf cart.)

5. The number and quality of prizes to be awarded is at the sole discretion of the tournament chairman. This rule is imposed in an attempt to thwart any profiteering by sand-

baggers, plants, impostors, and those who just plain lie through their teeth about their handicap.

6. *Cursing,* if properly done with force and dignity, under circumstances deemed appropriate by the tournament chairman, will be permitted. However, loud and boisterous cussing is strictly prohibited and will incur a severe reprimand by the mother of the bride (and wife of the tournament chairman).

7. You may purchase up to four mulligans (extra ball employed on any wayward shot) from the tournament chairman *before* the start of play. The price of each mulligan will depend on just how badly the participant wishes to win this tournament and help the tournament chairman defray the cost of the wedding. With reference to these mulligans, we are talking about big money.

8. In a sense of anticipation, one bar of imitation golf ball soap will be furnished each foursome just in case you may wish to lather up while retrieving your ball from the lake on three, eight, or twelve. Replacement bars will be furnished on the turn. (Soap courtesy of Bo Whaley.)

9. The white stakes to the left of the fairway on eighteen—out of bounds. The golf pro, Tommy Birdsong, lives in the fourth house on the left of eighteen from the eighteenth tee. I suggest you talk to him about your hook (if right-handed) or slice (if left-handed) while retrieving your ball from his yard. Also, beware of the dog behind the patio fence at the pro's house. He has been trained to commence barking on your back swing.

10. The proper and accepted warning cry to other golfers on the golf course is "Fore!" Not "Fo, y'all."

11. All play will be terminated at 12:30 P.M., the same day play begins. After all, three and one-half hours of frustration is enough for the groom on his wedding day. This will also provide sufficient time for tempers to cool before the wedding tee-off at 4:00 P.M.

12. Incomplete scores will be completed by the tournament chairman. Also, participants may use their charge-a-graft card to ensure a presentable score.

Part 4

Life Isn't What It Used to Be

There are those in our society who long for what they commonly refer to as "The good old days." I know we have such a man in our town, affectionately referred to by young and old as "Uncle Lunce." Uncle Lunce, who is just a few years older than baseball and the Olympics, steadfastly refuses to loosen his grip on the past. If I've heard him say it once, I must have heard him say it five hundred times, "I'll tell ya', boys—nostalgia ain't what it used to be."

I'm convinced Uncle Lunce is right in many respects, but wrong in others—like the IRS. The IRS theme never changes. "Get 'em!" is the name of the game. If they keep hounding me for the next fifteen years like they have the past fifteen, I may just pay 'em to get 'em off my back.

Travel has changed, though. Oh, how it has changed! It appears now that the airplane is making steady progress to replace the automobile, and in the next fifty years space ships will make people ask about those "old-fashioned airplanes" we used to ride in.

And we continue to dream, from childhood on up. Dreams don't change all that much with visions of romance and riches dominating the scene. No child can envision failure, and no mother ever gave birth to one. In the eyes of mothers, only successful children are born.

If you want to see life at its best and a young couple's patience tested to the fullest, just watch them build their first house. To escape divorce or aggravated manslaughter is a monumental achievement, and then comes the monthly payments that approach the national debt.

Every generation, I think, sees more change than the preceding one. And each says the same thing: "I just don't see how life can change any more."

But it does, every day.

The Annual IRS Armed Robbery

I'm convinced that taxpayers are far less aggravated by having to pay taxes than by the manner in which the Washington spendthrifts dole out the loot.

Every year we try to stick it to the IRS, with little success. But last year a little guy named Joe, who runs a small repair shop upstairs in his home, tried it with a different twist after losing an inexpensive claw hammer that sold for about $7.50 in any hardware store.

Joe recorded the loss: "One claw hammer. Value—$435."

Granted the hammer had a street value of $7.50, but Joe deferred to the wisdom of a higher authority, the Department of Defense, to determine replacement cost at current market value.

He began collecting news reports revealing how much the Pentagon had been paying for some of the same spare parts he used in his business. Joe also read that, according to the IRS, the value of inherited property is usually its *fair market value* at the time of the decedent's death rather than the property's original cost.

Plus, the IRS defines *fair market value* as "the price at which the property would exchange hands between a buyer and a seller. . . . Sales of similar property, on or about the same date, may be helpful in figuring the *fair market value* of the property."

Fair enough, Joe concluded.

Two weeks later, Joe suffered another mishap while remodeling a bathroom. A box wrench slipped from his hand, fell to the floor, and chipped. The wrench bounced off the new toilet seat and cracked the lid. And the round nut he'd been tightening rolled under the house, and he never found it.

Joe consulted his Pentagon Cost File to determine the *fair market value* of the wrench, toilet seat lid, and round nut and recorded in his ledger:

- Wrench: $469
- Toilet seat lid: $640.09
- Round nut: $2,043

A week later Joe's shop was robbed. Referring again to his Pentagon Cost File, he determined these *fair market value* replacement costs:

- Screws by the thousands: $37 apiece
- Four screwdrivers used to turn the $37-screws: $265 each
- Four toolboxes used to carry $37-screws and $265-screwdrivers: $652 each

The thieves also broke into Joe's pickup and stole:

- Two flashlights: $214 each
- Flat metal washers (100): $387 each
- Tape measure: $437

They also ransacked Joe's office, where he confronted them with a footstool and knocked one over his new sofa and chair and into his coffee maker. The damage prompted the replacement of the furniture's four armrest pads ($670.06 each) and the coffee maker ($7,622).

During the fight, Joe slammed the footstool into the wall when one of the thieves ducked, causing all three of the ($1,118 each) plastic footstool caps to pop off.

Having had enough, the thieves fled out the window and down Joe's adjustable aluminum ladder ($74,165), damaging it beyond repair.

By year's end, Joe's deductible losses were so high he owed *no* income tax. But the feds owed Joe a whopping refund.

Did Joe get his refund? Be serious, will you? What Joe pays for spare parts and what the Pentagon pays for same is as different as the Chinese AK-47 and the IRS-1040.

IRS Refund Checks Can Put a Fella' in the Hole

I would imagine that among the topics of conversation that dominate morning coffee tables and afternoon courthouse square benches in the spring are forms; not forms generally associated with beauty contests, Florida beaches, and some magazines—but IRS forms, 1040s.

I heard a Clemson economist elaborate on the preparation of his 1040 three years ago during a speech to the Dublin Rotary Club. He said, "I mailed my check to the IRS yesterday, and as I made it out I felt like the federal government had placed a pistol right between my eyes and robbed me." Thundering applause followed.

Then, there is the story of the IRS man who telephoned a preacher to ask if a certain affluent member of his congregation had in fact made a $10,000 contribution to the church building fund the previous year.

"No, he didn't," replied the preacher. "But I can assure you he will!"

Like anybody else who's ever fought the 1040 battle, I find the things to be a pain in the (you choose the appropriate anatomical spot).

In the first place, the instructions for filling out the aggravating things were no doubt prepared by Sesame Street students shortly before milk, cookie, and nap time, when they were in their worst possible mood. And, it's hard to draw up a set of 1040 instructions with one thumb in your mouth, the other in your ear, bubble gum in your hair, and standing in line on one foot while desperately waiting to get in the "baffroom."

In my 45 years of filling out the darn things, I've experienced no major problems—with one exception, 1968. That was the year that line 66 almost did me in.

My problem in '68 was that after fighting and cussing the 1040 for the better part of two nights and a rainy Sunday afternoon when it was too wet to play golf, I ended up qualifying for a $639 refund. Of course, that was back in the days of "Married, filing joint return," and two little exemptions named Joe and Lisa.

All finished, I couldn't wait until Monday morning to get that sucker in the mail. I drove to the post office in a rainstorm to drop it in the out-of-town slot. And not being quite sure of the required amount of postage, I licked and affixed five dollars worth of stamps to the upper right-hand corner of the envelope that contained my windfall. But, who cares about the paltry sum of five dollars when, within weeks, you're destined to become rich to the tune of $639.

Getting an IRS refund check is tantamount to hitting the jackpot on a Las Vegas quarter bandit, or the dime bandit that, in 1968, occupied (and probably still does) an honored (but secret) place on a shelf in the back room of (I'll Never Tell's) juke joint, about a six-pack south of Swainsboro on the Altamaha River.

How can a $639 tax refund be a problem? Read on.

On Monday morning, after having mailed my 1040 up to Chamblee (wherever the heck that is), I stopped in at Payne-Schwabe Buick in Swainsboro. They also sold Opels in 1968. Did I say I stopped in? Correction—I was waiting for Ed Schwabe when he unlocked the front door at 8:00 A.M.

"Know the little blue Opel Kadet my sixteen-year-old boy's been looking at, Ed?" I asked. "Well, roll it out. I'll take it."

Next, I waited for James Smith to unlock the front door at the Citizens Bank at 9:00 A.M. By 9:15 A.M., I'd signed a $3,000 note and my son Joe had his first car—a 1968 blue Opel Kadet.

"No problem," I assured Smith. "Got some money coming from the government soon."

In my feeble mind a $639 tax refund check certainly qualified me to blow $3,000 on an Opel. But I wasn't finished. No, I'd just started, and the stamps on my envelope to Chamblee weren't even dry yet.

My next stop was the Surrey Shop, a fine men's clothing store, where I cornered Gene Simmons and bought two sport coats, five pairs of trousers, and a batch of shirts—to be monogrammed, of course, with WWW on the pocket.

For years I had wanted me some of them monogrammed shirts like the doctors, lawyers, bankers, and bootleggers wore. So, with a bundle of cash on the way ($639), I loaded up. Total amount of my Surrey Shop purchases? A measley $435.

Well, sir, by the time my $639 government tax refund check arrived I had made purchases or obligations in the amounts of: $3,000 for a blue Opel Kadet; $435 for clothes; $55 for a pair of loafers; $265 for a new shotgun (to go with the six I already owned); $650 for a Rolex watch; $85 for a girl's bicycle; $185 for a trampoline; $850 for six root canals and porcelain caps.

Being a considerate and compassionate husband at the time, I also blew $27 on the wife—for a new set of kitchen knives. But had I known then what I know now I'd never have bought knives.

The total was $5,552 spent, based on an anticipated $639 tax refund check. And it took me five years to get my dumb head back above water.

Now, a request, IRS. Please! No more refund checks. I really can't afford one.

It Ain't Easy Keeping Up with the Joneses These Days

I don't care what anybody says, it just flat ain't as easy to keep up with the Joneses as it used to be. Time was when a fella could buy a new pair of overalls, have his wife turn the collar on his Sunday shirt, put a new coat of whitewash on his house and new oilcloth on the kitchen table, plant new petunias in the syrup cans, get the order off to Sears, and he'd be in th' runnin'. Not no more. Times have changed, and so have the things that give us that much-desired status, real or imagined. Like these image makers:

• *Cars:* If you ain't got a numbered car you ain't nothin', Jack. And sometimes even that won't get it if your number ain't big enough. Like you go rollin' up Walter and Edwina's circular driveway in your 220 an' you'll be directed to a parking area in back behind the utility building before you can say Dow-Jones or Rolex. On your way back there, take a quick look at the XJ6, 560SL, and 735i in their garage as you pass by—and try hard to explain to your wife why you have to park behind the utility building. This day and time a 220 just flat won't make the team.

I well remember joining an exclusive social club in Dublin about eight years ago. The wording in my letter of acceptance as composed by the head honcho at the time, David Baggett, read thisaway:

> Dear Bo:
> I am pleased to inform you that your application for membership has been approved, with one major restriction. It is respectfully requested that when attending the club for any function, please park your car in the rear of the building, behind the Dempsey Dumpster. Welcome to the club!
> Your brother, David.

My car? I was sporting a 1965 Mercury Marauder at the time. Some of you know her affectionately as "Maude," and she has no number but is pretty familiar with 10W40 to the tune of five quarts every 300 miles.

I really didn't realize until I paid a visit not long ago to friends who live on Lusty Lane in Dunwoody just how important numbered cars are. Would you believe that there's a guy, his wife, and eighteen-month-old son living in a house there with a two-and-a-half car garage that houses his 450SLC, her 300ZX, and the kid's tricycle—a TR—1½?

On the other hand, I have a good friend in Dublin who owns a 300D and one of those four-wheel drive Broncos. Plus his wife has a nice Buick. None of the vehicles ever make it inside the garage. No room. It is filled with loot his pretty wife lugs home from yard sales around the country. Just imagine, more than $50,000 worth of cars sit outside in the rain, ice, sleet, snow, and blistering sunshine in deference to $23.85 worth of junk.

If Joe could just convince Ruth (no last names, please) to load her loot in his Bronco and dump it in the dumpster where I park, then maybe at least two of the vehicles could spend a couple of peaceful and safe days and nights in the garage.

• *Real Estate:* If you really want to get in trouble, try this. Just contract to have a builder construct your dream house over on Passion Place, say with roughly 4,300 square feet of living space, and let your wife, Candi, find out that the Astorbilts are building one across the street with 4,650 square feet of living space. And you bought your rocks for the front of the house from up near Tate while the Astorbilts had theirs custom cut in the south of France.

You have two choices, Irving. Either add 351 square feet to your floor plan and book a flight to the south of France, or file for divorce—whichever is cheaper.

Landscaping is a vital factor, too. Don't dare have the yard man plant 347 red tulips only to find out that the Astorbilts had 351 set out. How would that sound at the club? "You know what, Myrtle? That stupid Irving only ordered 347 red tulips while Wally and Jane Astorbilt have 351!"

Of course, there just has to be a conversation piece in the den. A bulldozer would be nice, but sure as hell the Astorbilts would come on strong with a front-end loader or a backhoe. A Heisman Trophy would be nice, but the supply is limited.

Of course, Irving could just throw caution to the wind and, like way-out architect John Portman did, roll in a Delta 757 and paint a sign on the fuselage stating, "We're Ready When You Are."

I have the feeling that Candi would like that, and what could the Astorbilts do to top it? Build a PTL water slide or an Oral Roberts prayer tower? Maybe stand Joe Frank Harris in front of the fireplace? He'll be available before long.

• *Education:* Don't underestimate the prestige of the school your children attend. Stand your ground when defending the merits of the school of your child's choice.

Like the two women, Tina and Corky, who were sipping margaritas by the pool one summer afternoon and became engaged in a heated argument about this very subject:

"Well, I can tell you one thing!" screamed Corky. "It's a known fact that my son flunked out of a better school than yours did!"

Just remember this: don't take a back seat to nobody when it comes to status. Just last week I was talkin' with my friend Ross Shepherd as we devoured a few delicious hot dogs at Shinholster's Minute Grill, located next to Ross's barbershop.

"Well, I'll jus' tell ya', Ross," I mumbled between bites. "I've known that family for years an' all of 'em are very affluent."

"Oh, yeah? Well, I don't care what their religion is, I like 'em anyway," Ross allowed.

Little Things Cause the Most Trouble

What's wrong with the world? I'm not sure, but every morning I listen to a front-table group of pseudo-intellectuals debate the question.

They debate such issues as inflation, the economy, the plight of the American farmer, Social Security, the federal budget, and nuclear arms. But these aren't the issues that drive you frantic day in and day out, produce sleepless nights, and cause divorces.

Rather, it's the nagging little things that cause all the trouble, little things like nothing is made right anymore, and nothing fits. Furniture comes apart when a special guest sits down, and zippers get stuck (down) less than a minute before a scheduled speech before the local garden club or the Business and Professional Women's Club of Willacoochee.

Television programming has gone to pot. The one program you've looked forward to watching for weeks is postponed to make way for a documentary on Icelandic fishing and its importance to world economics.

People aren't reliable these days, either. Like the girl who promised you faithfully that she'd be there at noon to help out with your daughter's reception, but calls at 11:45 A.M. to tell you she can't come because she's taking part in a mass baptism or attending a meeting of the part-time maid's association to vote on whether to affiliate with the Teamsters.

It's things like this that warp the world. You buy one of those TV discs that bring in 784 channels, only to have the neighbor's dog chew the wire and instead of watching the finals of the Miss World Contest in Miami on the Playboy channel, the screen flashes a rerun of sumo wrestling in Yokohama on ESPN.

Here are some other things that can bug a fella' to the point of climbing on top of Dublin's skyscraper at South Jefferson and Madison, and shouting to all of America, "I'm mad as hell! And I'm not gonna' take it any more!" Like these:

• *Warranties:* They always take care of anything except what happens. Like when you take your new garden hose home and hook it up. The thing spurts water in every direction *except* in the direction of the rose bushes, for which you bought it. This is not covered. What *is* covered is that the hose won't ever shrink or straighten out.

• *Medical insurance.* Whatever the doctor tells me has to be done, the policy specifically exempts. You have to catch the disease *they* want.

• *Buttons:* Somebody, somewhere, is going to get rich doing nothing but matching buttons. Ever try to match a button on your blazer? They don't make them. Sometimes you take your new blazer home and, as you button the second button, your finger goes right through the hole with the button on the end—of your finger. Is it so hard to sew on blazer buttons and reinforce them? Not for you, but for manufacturers it is seemingly impossible. A strong wind will blow them off. BUT . . . just try and remove the tag on the sleeve that identifies the size of your blazer and see what happens. It takes a crowbar, the strength of Paul Anderson, and the patience of Job to do it. If only the buttons were sewn on as well. . . .

• *Kitchen utensils.* There's the nifty knife sharpener that makes a saw out of your favorite carving knife; the stainless steel flatware that turns gray; the self-cleaning oven. Hah! My oven is just as dingy and grimy as when I moved in last July. What about other kitchen items, like free-flowing salt that nothing can prevent from coming out except the slightest humidity in the air. And the improved ketchup bottle that produces no ketchup until you bang it on the table, run hot water on its neck, stick a gray stainless steel knife down its throat causing a flow of oooozzzy tomato stuff to run down your arm.

Whipped cream pressure cans? No problem. Just shake them like the instructions say and thick, luscious, imitation whipped cream squirts all over the cabinets, the wall, the dog, a sampling of children, and two or three chairs.

Pickle jars with the easy-to-get-off lids are simple. Just take three different kinds of can openers, vice-grip pliers, a screwdriver, one of those rubberized grabbers and see if you can beat the machine that welded the lid on.

Then, there is the company that sends your bill with the reminder that "If not paid by the 10th, we will tell your mother-in-law," along with a self-addressed envelope for your remittance—and the remittance won't fit in the envelope.

What's wrong with the world? I'm not real sure, but a relative newcomer has joined the world of child-proof medicine bottles, glass patio doors, and television commercials: the computer.

You know about computers. They're the little devils that conspire against writers annndd do dheir ded-lebel bes tu messs up anithing ad eberthengg yu tri tu rite.

Inventors Who Ought to Be Hanged

I'm convinced that certain products are designed, manufactured, and marketed not for convenience, but strictly to aggravate. Take a look at these, for example:

• *Wire Coathangers*. The darn things breed, right? Hang half a dozen straight as a West Point parade line in your closet tonight then check 'em first thing in the morning. They'll be there, all twenty-three of 'em, as twisted and tangled as Bo Derek's hair. (But they'll look a heck of a lot better.)

• *Toll Booths*. This is what usually happens at toll booths:

You're beat after driving seven solid hours with Willie Kate up front and the kids, eight and six, back in the tourist section.

You haven't passed up a rest room or a McDonald's this side of New Jersey. A monotonous white line has been the scenery from the New Jersey Turnpike to the Sunshine Parkway while you routinely, almost subconsciously, threw away more quarters than a female slot machine addict in Las Vegas.

Suddenly, there it is! Toll Booth Ahead—Cars With Exact Change Use Right Lane says the big sign with white letters. So, you make your move; so do 387 other Florida-bound chauffeurs.

One-handed, you steer toward the wide-mouthed monster that eats quarters, only quarters, while fumbling in your right pants pocket. All the while the back-seat tourists are chorusing a too-familiar refrain. "Let me, Daddy! Let me throw it in! It's my turn!"

Do you have a quarter? No sale. The Coke machine at the I-75 rest area eighty-five miles back cleaned you out. Willie Kate? Don't be ridiculous! She hasn't had one since Six Flags.

So you're trapped in the exact change lane while the monster waits with open mouth. The line of cars behind resembles a presidential motorcade and sounds like New Year's Eve at Times Square. There you sit with six pennies, two nickels, a dime, two subway tokens, a book of McDonald's matches, and a nail clipper, none of which will get you past the monster without lights, bells, buzzers and sirens signaling to all that you cheated!

• *Automobile Hood Release Thingamajigs*. Right here is where we need some legislation. Never mind constitutional revision and supplemental budgets. Let's get on with important stuff, like mandating that hood release thingamajigs be located in the same place on all cars. Where are they now? Inside, outside, in the grille, over the grille, under the grille, over the bumper, under the bumper, you name it, Mr. Goodwrench. Why? Because the automobile manufacturers are in cahoots with the nail clipper people, that's why.

Ever had car trouble late at night seventeen miles from nowhere, with steam spewing from the radiator like a vigorously shaken Coke, and you try to find the hood release thingamajig? Forget it! You'll have more luck finding a crew cut and a pair of saddle oxfords on U.S. 441 on a Sunday afternoon.

• *A Few More Mind-Bogglers.* I've previously vented my frustrations regarding a few other aggravating gadgets. Like those cute little triangular coffee creamers that spurt artificial cream in every direction except your coffee cup. And those individual mustard and catsup takeouts that are as unpredictable as a woman. Just try putting the yellow and red on your hot dog and see what happens. You end up with both on your bifocals and all over your Timex.

Then there's the one that literally drives me up the restaurant wall: deformed table legs. Ever sit at a table with deformed legs? You must have.

You sit on one side, she sits on the other. You pick up your glass and the table tilts toward her. She picks hers up and it tilts toward you. Only two ways to correct it.

First, practice until you both lift your glasses at the same time. That's a lot of fun and it does give you a feeling of togetherness.

Second, you try everything on the table: folded paper napkins, match covers, saucer, ash tray, a couple of butter patties, and the cap off the catsup bottle. You try, usually unsuccessfully, to make an adjustment by easing the item that most nearly fits under the deformed leg. (Of course, you should expect to tip over a water glass or cup of coffee in the process; that's precisely what the manufacturer had in mind when the legs were sawed.) You can always move to another table and insult the couple at the next one by so doing.

The ultimate pest? Safety medicine bottles. No doubt in my mind, they were invented by a sadist. Just try to open one at 2:00 A.M., in the dark, without your glasses. The thing is definitely an offshoot of one of the most frustrating items ever to come on the market: the combination lock! Grant me three minutes to share a recent experience I had with one:

I had played golf with a friend and rode in his golf cart. Following my usual routine, I removed my watch and placed it in the cart tray along with old tees and dead birdies.

We finished the round, I paid off, and went home. It was 9:00 P.M. before I missed my watch. I heard the time on the radio. I only knew it was Thursday, A.D., and that's close enough for the schedule I follow. I called my friend, explained what I'd done, and asked if I could get the key to his cart stall.

"I'd rather go without my jockey shorts than my watch," I told him.

"No problem. You don't need a key. My cart shed has a combination lock. I'll just give you the combination," he said.

"Fine, go ahead," I told him.

"O.K. Here's what you do. You can't miss. Turn the dial two times to the right and stop on 14. Got that?"

"Gotcha'," I replied.

"Next, turn one time to the left past 14 and on to 4. Stop on 4. Got it?"

"No problem. Stop on 4," I echoed.

"O.K. Then, turn back right to 30 and pull. That's all there is to it," he assured me.

All there is to it? Read on.

This was the one night it's rained in Dublin since World War II. No problem, though, I thought. I'd just zip on out to the country club, twist that little ol' dial a few times, get my watch, and return home.

In the first place, I couldn't see. I barely found the lock, much less the dadgummed dial. Finally, I began twisting and turning while squinting through foggy bifocals.

I tried it on two legs, then standing on one. Tongue in, tongue out. With and without profanity. Twist and pull; twist and pull. I out-twisted Chubby Checker and out-pulled a Wisconsin dairy farmer. Did the lock open? Heck no, it didn't open! I'd have had more success uncoupling a freight car.

I sounded like a quarterback, standing there in the dark, twisting and mumbling, "Right 14! Left 4! Right 30! Pull!" Nothing!

No doubt about it, friend. It takes more than the combination to open one of those monsters, and whatever it takes, I didn't have it. I took the easy way out; I gave up and went home. Oh, my watch? I went with my friend and got it the next day. He opened the lock in less than fifteen seconds.

"See? No problem," he said, gloating.

Oh, yeah? Well, I'd like to see him open the hood of my car without breaking a fingernail on the hood release thingamajig. No way. Absolutely no way.

Who Is Making All These Wrong Number Calls after Midnight?

Ahhh! The wonderful world of the telephone. That little sucker can be a wonderful companion, or a pain in the receiver, right?

Some people literally live with a telephone receiver glued to their ear. In fact, my daughter was fifteen before I found out there wasn't a big, black thing growing out of her left ear.

I've never figured out why my telephone is programmed to ring as soon as I step into the shower and get my eyes filled with soap, I'm out in the yard cleaning my motorcycle or up to my armpits cleaning fish, or waiting in the den for a 47-yard field goal attempt with nine seconds remaining in the Georgia-Clemson game and the score tied 21-21.

And answer me this, Ma Bell. Why do the wrong number calls always come at my house after midnight but never at ten in the morning or three in the afternoon? Answer me that, please ma'am.

Another mystery to me is why Information operators are always in such a hurry. Do they work on production like the women at Oxford Manufacturing, who sew on buttons or make button holes? I mean, what's their hurry? Where the heck are they going? The way I figure it, if they have to put in eight hours they might as well talk to me as anybody else.

You know how it goes. You dial 1-215-555-1212 to get a Philadelphia number from the Information operator. And they always start out so friendly, like this:

Rrrrrnnnggg! Rrrrnnnggg!

"Hello, this is Bertha. What city, please?"

"Well, hey there, Bertha! This here's Bo, in Dublin, Georgia. How's y'r mama 'n 'em, and—?"

"What city did you wish, please?" she interrupts impatiently.

"Weeellll! 'Scuse me, Bertha," you whimper.

Your feelings fractured and your ego dangling down around your ankles, you dial and try again.

Rrrrnnnggg! Rrrrnnnggg!

"Hello, this is Phyllis. What city, please?"

"Oh, uh, hey there, Phyllis! This here's Bo, in Dublin, Georgia. How's Bertha 'n 'em—".

"What city did you wish, please?" she asks impatiently, like maybe she has a roast in the oven at home, or better yet, a pot of Hamburger Helper.

"Well, to tell you th' truth, Phyllis, I was sorta' lookin' f'r the City of Brotherly Love, but I dang sure dialed th' wrong number. 'Scuse th' ring, please," you say and hang up.

Hurry, hurry, hurry! The Information operators are always in a dadgummed hurry. They start out friendly enough, but they're always in a hurry.

Hollywood's Version of Air Travel Just Ain't So!

Several months ago I saw about ten minutes of a Gregory Peck–June Allyson movie on Channel 2. Briefly, this is what I saw:

Gregory Peck was seated in a lounge chair by the swimming pool in his back yard, sipping on whatever a movie star sips on when sitting by his swimming pool. June Allyson, his movie wife, was in the kidney-shaped pool.

Shortly, the sound of a telephone ringing in the distance invaded the tranquility of this poolside utopia. Within seconds, a Japanese houseboy appeared on the scene with a white telephone attached to a three-mile cord. He bowed and almost apologetically said to Peck, "Long distance for you, Mr. Morrison." Then he placed the telephone on a nearby table and skipped off. (Japanese houseboys always "skip off.")

Peck's telephone conversation was brief. He hung up the receiver and said to June, "I have to be in New York in the morning for a board meeting at ten o'clock. I'll have to catch a plane out this afternoon. Can you drive me to the airport, dear?"

"Certainly, darling," June cooed.

The next scene on the screen showed Peck sitting in the passenger seat of a sleek convertible with the top down, and June Allyson driving toward the airport on a picture postcard highway with the ocean in the background.

The next scene had June parking right in front of the terminal. She and Peck walked to the boarding gate where she kissed him before he disappeared in a tunnel. She moved to a window to await the take-off so she could blow a kiss in the general direction of a giant 747.

Meanwhile, the camera zeroed in on Peck as he entered the airplane to settle down in his first-class seat. Shortly, a girl who looked like Miss Venezuela and on her way to the Miss Universe Pageant slid into the seat next to him. The seat on the other side of him was occupied by Morganna, on her way to disrupt the World Series.

At LaGuardia Airport, Miss Venezuela and Morganna deplaned and walked through the terminal to waiting taxicabs. Peck is next shown in the board room of a large corporation where he is presiding over a meeting of the board of directors. The clock on the wall behind him shows 10:10 A.M.

That's the Hollywood version of air travel. But friends and neighbors, that just ain't the way it is. The Hollywood script writers left out a few important details. Let me write the script and show it like it really is.

• Why don't they show June Allyson saying, "Take you to the airport? Are you off your gourd? I have an aerobics class with Jane Fonda in forty-five minutes."

• Why don't they show Peck scrounging all over the house looking for clean underwear and shirts?

• Why don't they show June Allyson getting behind a school bus or an army convoy on the way to the airport?

• Why don't they show Gregory Peck fighting his way through a regiment of Japanese exchange students, each with a Nikon hanging around his neck and a souvenir ditty bag from the Atlanta Chamber of Commerce hanging from his shoulder, trying to get to the Delta ticket agent?

• Why don't they show Peck and Allyson walking for miles, and running at full speed the last two, to get to the boarding gate?

• Why don't they show Peck taking a seat back next to the food storage compartment and the toilet?

• Why don't they show an old gal that resembles a mud slide wiggle and grunt to get into her seat next to Peck's?

• Why don't they show Peck standing in front of the baggage carousel at LaGuardia nervously awaiting his two-suiter and overnight bag that never make the turn?

• Why don't they show the look of disgust on Peck's face when he's told that his baggage at that very moment "is on its way to Dallas"?

• Why don't they show Peck standing in the rain in front of the LaGuardia terminal frantically trying to hail a taxi-cab, along with a regiment of Japanese exchange students?

• Why don't they show Peck trying unsuccessfully to explain to a cab driver who recently arrived in New York from Haiti that he doesn't want to go to Yankee Stadium, he wants to go to the Americana Hotel?

Truth in writing? They ain't got it in Hollywood!

Few Childhood Dreams Ever Become Realities

Childhood aspirations don't always work out, do they? Like the eight-year-old who planned to be a fireman, but ended up teaching high school math; the ten-year-old who had his heart set on preaching great sermons and leading world-wide crusades but now, at fifty-two, operates a bulldozer; or the twelve-year-old who just knew she'd be another Florence Nightingale and administer to the sick, but spends her time now, thirty-three years later, taking orders and serving food.

Most of us had childhood dreams—like performing surgery in a large hospital, delivering that classic argument before the U.S. Supreme Court, or designing skyscrapers that would dwarf the Peachtree Center Hotel in Atlanta, the Empire State Building in New York, or the Woolworth Building in Chicago.

How many of the dreams materialized? Few, probably.

"Rich Man, Poor Man. . . ."

As a boy, I guess I ran the gamut of professional aspirations. I dreamed of being everything—rich man, poor man, beggar man, thief; doctor, lawyer, Indian chief. I had a profession for each day of the week . . . and always a preacher on Sunday.

I must have been about six when I made my first big decision as to how I'd spend my life. No doubt about it, I'd be a preacher. My daddy was one and the job appealed to me as it would any six-year-old.

After all, what other job allows a man to hunt and fish whenever he pleases? Not to mention constantly being invited to free fried chicken suppers, complete with homemade pies and cakes. And that looked pretty doggone good to a six-year-old who loved to hunt and fish and dearly loved fried chicken, homemade pies and cakes.

"For Better or Worse"

My first official act as a self-proclaimed pastor at the ripe old age of six was to perform the marriage ceremony for Jack Smith, six, and his seven-year-old bride, Frances Courson, behind the Methodist church in Alma. A reception followed featuring vanilla wafers, popsicles, and Kool-Aid.

Jack and Frances remained man and wife for about three hours, until Robert Boyd, eight, lured Frances away from Jack with a handful of bubble gum.

Fickle! That Frances Courson was just downright fickle!

Shortly after Jack and Frances separated, I moved to Oglethorpe, left the pulpit, and became a doctor.

My hero was Dr. Derrick, and the fact that he was a veterinarian was of no consequence to me. Everybody called him "Doctor," and that was good enough for me.

Early in my brief medical career I had a patient named Aloysius, the skinniest mule in Macon County, Georgia. You could read a newspaper through him, and he had undoubtedly the sharpest backbone of any mule ever. Have you experienced the thrill of riding a skinny mule, with a razor-sharp backbone, bareback? Like sitting on a rail on a railroad track, and no matter how many times you shift from right to left, left to right, that rail is still there.

I treated Aloysius for everything from hernia to hemorrhoids, puncturing him with Mama's sewing needles and rubbing yellow salve all over him, but he died anyway; and I became a preacher again, officiating at his funeral. And while there just ain't a whole lot to be said about a skinny mule with a razor-sharp backbone, I tried. But if mules go to heaven, Aloysius is there.

Next, at age ten, I became a thief—a train and bank robber. This was after I'd seen Tyrone Power (Jesse) and Henry Fonda (Frank) in *The Jesse James Story* at the Montezuma picture show. My gang rode stick horses the two miles from Montezuma to Oglethorpe and up to the front door of the make-believe bank (actually, a junk shed behind the parsonage), took all the money, and rode off on our "horses" to the James gang's hideaway up over the garage at C.L. Barfield's house. We must have stashed more than a million dollars up there before giving up bank robbing to go straight. I became a lawyer and C.L. became a truck driver.

Anyway, even with all the bank money we stole and stashed up over C.L.'s garage, we didn't have a nickel for a belly-washer. But that's the way it is with bank robbers—feast or famine.

A short time later I saw another movie, a "shoot-'em-up" starring Wild Bill Elliott who must have killed a million Indians—but not Cochise. So, I became an Indian chief and tried to scalp one of Mama's hens—a definite mistake.

"Heap big Indian chief no mess with white woman's chickens," she said after capturing me.

Part 5

Rednecks, White Trash, and Juke Joints

There are many things on which I am not an authority, but rednecks, white trash, and juke joints ain't among them. These I know about because I was raised within elbow-rubbing distance from all three. Each is in a class by itself, and there is a caste system prevalent among them.

Rednecks are a proud and cocky lot. Male and female, they'll fight you at the drop of a longneck Bud bottle. They require little of life's luxuries, and their allegiance is to their mamas and daddies, even unto death. They hang out at their own special juke joints, and status is instant when they enter with their personalized cue sticks for the nightly game of eight-ball, with head-busting to follow.

I once heard male rednecks described by a female counterpart as being "a bunch who think they're ladies' men, but ain't. Heck, most of 'em couldn't get a date in a women's prison with a handful of pardons."

Blue jeans, western boots and shirts, pickup trucks, and Levi Garrett chewing tobacco are their trademarks. Plus they know every country song to come out of Nashville since Roy Acuff first bellowed out "Wabash Cannonball."

White trash are a different lot. They ain't been nowhere, ain't going nowhere, and don't give a hoot about going nowhere. Their knowledge seldom extends beyond where to get anything free, where to sign up for government assistance, and where the best place is to get a handout.

To give credit where credit is due, however, I must admit that there are a few who actually know the names of all their children and what school, if any, they attend. Birthdays are another kettle of fish, however. They are just things that happen, like birth about every eleven months.

Juke joints are the same to rednecks and white trash as country clubs are to those who have showered, shaved, and secured a regular job. They will get up off their sick bed to crawl down to the "juke" and play the pinball machine or a few George Jones selections. Employment is something that is done just long enough to qualify for unemployment compensation, and they know the postman's schedule on check day better than he does.

These folks are a breed all their own. Their one desire is to be left alone to do their thing independent of such trivia as law enforcement, paying taxes, and voting. Such nonsense is within the bailiwick of the country club set as far as they are concerned.

Motto? Certainly, they have one: "Speak loudly, and carry a sharp knife!'

A Hall of Fame Type of Juke Joint

Over the past four years I've made frequent trips to Alabama. I don't think there's a truck stop or juke joint in the state that I haven't visited at least once. Like a required course in college, Bonnie's Bar and Beauty Shop, somewhere in the vicinity of Boaz, should be a required stop for anybody traveling through, or visiting, the state.

I first heard about Bonnie's in 1986 from a Waycross trucker named Gator at a truck stop in Cullman. My books are sold there and he'd bought one, *Rednecks and Other Bonafide Americans,* on a previous stop. Clyde, the truck stop manager, introduced us.

"Please t' meet'cha," he said. "I had me a bunch o' fun witcha' book. An' that Robbie Nell Bell, from Alma (Robbie Nail Bail, fum Almer) is somethin' else, ain't she?"

"You got that right," I concurred.

"I tell ya, that gal kin ride with me anytime," he said. "She *is* real, ain't she?"

"As real as dirt and boiled peanuts," I told him.

"An' she's a big beer drinker?"

"Robbie Nell never met a beer she didn't like," I assured him. "She's got more beer cans in the back seat of her TransAm than a recycling plant. If she ever cleans out her car and sells 'em she'll be filthy rich," I said. "I figure she gets about sixty-eight miles to the six-pack."

Gator told me about Bonnie's, a hall of fame-type juke joint.

"I been a road jockey f'r eighteen years an' I ain't never seen nothin' like it. Heck, the fus' night I went there I got in three fights. Won two of 'em," he said.

"And the third?"

"Ol' gal name o' Dolly done me in with a pool stick when I tol' her she daintzed like a elephant an' smelled like a pig. Tha's whur these scars come fum," he said, pointing to an area around his left eye and ear.

"Where is it?"

"Out fum Boaz," he said. "Jus' go south a few miles to the big oak tree an' hang a lef'. Then look f'r th' pickups an' eighteen-wheelers."

"Thanks, I'll try it."

"Can't git in 'thout bein' recommended. Tell Bonnie I sentcha', but watch aout f'r Dolly. She dang near killed an insurance 'juster fum Montgomery las' summer when he canceled Willie Nelson (J-8) on the jukebox and played Dolly Parton (M-6). She flat don't like Dolly Parton, or nobody else whut's lean an' purty."

Last year I started to walk in just as a fella' in a wheelchair came flying out the front door, thanks to Cody and Doc, two regulars. Man and wheelchair came flying through the air and landed next to a motorcycle.

Why was he evicted? "For fightin'," Cody said. "Bonnie don't allow no fightin' 'fore dark."

Over the years I've come to know the regulars well, like on a "Gimme a cigarette," "Put a quarter in the jukebox," and "Wanna' daintz, Sugah?" basis. One, especially, knocks me out. Name's Shorty, a poker playing, beer drinking, river fishing ne'er do well whose proudest accomplishment, by his own admission, is never having worked a day in his life. "I'm forty-four and ain't never hit a lick at a snake. I'm the only man in Alabama what ain't got no Social Security card, and don't want one. Go on record with the gov'mint an' they gotcha'. I don't need that."

Shorty, Buck, and Cooter spend more time at Bonnie's than Dan Quayle spends at the golf course.

"Where's Shorty?" I asked Cooter.

"Who knows? We ain't seen 'im since that encyclopedia selling gal hit town in March," Cooter allowed sorrowfully. "Once he seen her he got plumb moon-eyed an' even quit drinkin', gamblin', an' fishin'. Shorty ain't popped a top, drawed a card, or wet a hook in six months, and I hear tell he's goin' to church with her regular. I tell ya', let a fella' git struck by a woman and fum then on he jus' ain't worth a damn fer nothin'. I seen his two bird dogs las' week an' they's mopin' 'round somethin' awful. They prolly think ol' Shorty's done had a stroke."

"Tha's right," Buck agreed. "Nex' thing ya' know he'll git a dang job, start eatin' reg'lar, an' bathin'. Th' handwritin's on th' wall."

Too bad Shorty didn't come down with mumps or measles. They can be cured, but let a man become moon-eyed over a woman and he's had it. It's terminal.

Redneck in Flight

I knew it was going to be a fun flight when I arrived at the boarding gate in Atlanta to check in and select a seat on Delta Flight 436 to New Orleans. How did I know that? Because of those in line ahead of me, especially a good ol' boy from South Georgia and six Israelis.

The Israelis zoomed through with ease, assisted by the female gate attendant who was undoubtedly of New York extraction. The good ol' boy from South Georgia was about

thirty, six foot, four inches, and 225 pounds, thick blond
hair and TFV commercial teeth, wearing a faded plaid shirt
with two pockets (one holding a pouch of Levi Garrett and
the other assorted papers), well-worn Levis, no belt,
scuffed Dingo boots, and a beat-up black cap with STP on
it. He held a white styrofoam cup in his right hand and his
plane ticket to New Orleans in his left, periodically lifting
the cup to his lips. And he was happy and carefree.

I listened closely to this exchange between him and the
attendant:

"Your name, sir?"

"R.T.," he told her. "R.T. Howard."

"I need your full name, sir."

"That's it, Sugah," he said smiling. "They ain't no more.
Jus' plain R.T. Howard."

"What does the R.T. stand for, Mr. Howard?"

"Don' stan' f'r nuthin', ma'am. Tha's jus' my name, R.T.
Like yore name tag says 'M.W. Walker.' Does 'M.W. stand
f'r somethin'?"

She gave up and moved along with the interrogation.

"May I see your ticket, Mr. Howard?"

"Yessum, I got it rat cheer."

"Hmmmm . . . you're from Unadilla, Georgia?"

"Shore am, Route 1, Uner," he said smiling. "Lived there
all my life 'cept when I—"

"And you're flying to Noo Arleuns?"

"Right as rain, Sugah. New OrLeens, Loueasyanner! An'
I ain't never been on no airplane 'fore. I'm goin' to see my
li'l sister's new baby girl. Borned las' Tuesday mornin'
baout daylight. I's feedin' th' hawgs when my daddy tol' me
'baout it. My li'l sister, name's Wanda Sue, lives in Slidell
seein' as how—"

"Very good. I hope Wanda Sue and the baby will get
along fine. Now then, smoking or nonsmoking section?"

"What'cha mean, Sugah?"

"Your seat on the airplane. Do you prefer smoking or
nonsmoking?"

"Well, if'n hits all th' same to you I jus' as soon sit in th' no smokin' section 'cause if a big ol' airplane is gonna' smoke I ain't real innersted in watchin' it."

"I wasn't referring to the airplane. Do you smoke?"

"Shoot naw! I chew. My daddy'd tan my hide if'n he ever heered tell o' me a' smokin' cigarettes."

"Well, there's no chewing section on the airplane and be-sides—"

"Izat so? Well, you jus' don't worry none 'baout that, Sugah. They'll be one soon's I git on it. Thank ya', ma'am . . . an' y'all have a nice day, you heah?"

As soon as I boarded the airplane, I spotted R.T. seated across the aisle from me and two seats up in the chewing section, cup in hand. He was busily checking out the gadgets on the overhead panel, things like the oxygen mask, air vent, light switch, and the stewardess button.

We hadn't been airborne ten minutes when R.T. chose to give the stewardess button a try. He pushed it and called out loud and clear, "Brang me two doubles all the way, a order of Franch fries an' a big Coke with lotsa' ice!"

Like I said, I knew from the beginning it was going to be a fun flight.

It was inevitable that somewhere between Atlanta and New Orleans I would sit and talk with R.T. It happened over Montgomery and we talked until the plane touched down at the New Orleans airport. I initiated the conversation with a question:

"I heard you say you're from Unadilla. Do you know Tommy Kersey?"

"Shoot I reckon! You know ol' Tommy?"

"Just slightly."

"I've knowed 'im all my life. Heck, my daddy learned him how to drive a tractor. Ya' goin' to New OrLeens?"

"Right."

"Ya' fum there?"

"No, just going down there to the Superdome and—"

"Oh yeah? Goin' to a football game?"

"Sort of. More like a preseason game."

"Who's playin'?"

"The Republican Elephants and the Democratic Donkeys. They play every four years, second Tuesday in November."

"Who won las' time?"

"The Elephants. No contest."

"What wuz th' score?"

"Something like 54,455,075 to 37,577,185."

"Dang! Wud'n even close. Big crowd?"

"About ninety-two million, and there were more than sixty million no-shows."

"Them Elephants musta' played a heckuva' game."

"Yeah, they dominated both sides of the line all day. And the Elephant quarterback, Reagan, had his best day."

"Reagan? I've heard o' him 'fore. Name's Ron Reagan, ain't it? An' wuzn't he at Notter Dame?"

"Right, briefly. In fact, he got his start there about fifty years ago."

"Who was the quarterback for the Donkeys?"

"Some kid named Mondale. But he was out of his class. Dropped out of sight after the game. Hasn't been heard from since."

"How 'baout Reagan? He still playin'?"

"Sort of. This is his last year. He'll be retiring in January, the twentieth to be exact. Just can't remember the plays anymore. Calls for the hit and run when it's third and one on the eight, things like that. Called for a bunt last year when it was fourth and twenty-third on his own twelve."

"Tha's a dadgummed shame!" R.T. allowed. "Well, looks like we're a' gittin' ready to land. Nice talkin' to ya', an' have a nice time at th' Superdome."

"Thanks. Want me to walk with you to get your luggage?"

"Luggage? Did'n brang none."

"No luggage?"

"Nope. Heck, I ain't gonna' be heah but a week."

R.T. does travel light, just Levi Garrett and a styrofoam cup.

I watched R.T. as he gave a big "Bye, y'all!" to the stewardess, a cute girl from Georgia who was standing at the exit ramp. And I also heard her bid farewell to the six Israelis. While she didn't speak their language, or they hers, communication was no problem. Both came through loud and clear:

"So long!" she said to them with a southern smile.

"Shalom!" the Israelis called back in unison.

White Trash and Social Outcasts

And here they are, Ludlow Porch's White Trash Guidelines, along with Ten Ways to Become a Social Outcast, taken with permission from *Who Cares About Apathy?* Peachtree Publishers, 1987:

1. A recent survey has shown that white trash makes up 87.9 percent of the U.S. toothpick market.

2. White trash prefers to use their front porches to store discarded kitchen appliances.

3. The first three words white trash children learn to say are, "mama," "daddy," and "s——," not necessarily in that order.

4. White trash considers abandoned cars to be an important part of their landscape architecture.

5. White trash children must start smoking by age twelve.

6. White trash considers chickens to be household pets.

7. White trash are taught from infancy to talk with their mouth full of food while gesturing with whatever eating utensil may be handy at the moment.

8. White trash only park in handicapped parking spaces.

9. White trash are the exclusive market for white-side-wall-tire planters.

10. While all white trash are not wife beaters, all wife beaters are white trash.

11. The code of white trash requires that any of them attending a sporting event must be intoxicated prior to the end of the national anthem.

12. Seventy-eight percent of white trash have been fingerprinted by their seventeenth birthday.

13. White trash must have at least one relative named for an animal, such as Buck, Gator, or Hoss.

14. While there are rare exceptions, white trash will not marry blood relatives closer than nieces and nephews.

15. White trash consider man's best friend not to be the dog, but the jumper cable.

16. The white trash community cannot understand why a professional wrestler has never been appointed to the Supreme Court.

17. White trash consider any pickup with lawn furniture in the back to be a limo.

18. When white trash tell you they're self-educated, it means they read the *National Enquirer* every week.

19. The cars of white trash will not run without some fuzzy object hanging from the rearview mirror.

20. White trash men all refer to their wives as "my ol' lady."

White trash are not all bad and over the years some have risen to great heights. Two have appeared in Robert L. Ripley's "Believe It or Not"—one for being an only child and the other for having liability insurance on his car.

Here are Ten Ways to Become a Social Outcast:

1. Always interrupt. This lets people know that what you have to say is much more important than what they are saying.

2. Wear your hat while eating. This will brand you at best a clod, and at worst third generation white trash.

3. Comment on people's physical characteristics. Short people don't know they're short, and fat people don't know they're fat. They must depend on jerks like you to tell them.

4. Never say "Thank you" or "I'm sorry," signs of good upbringing, and you don't want to be cursed with that stigma.

5. Blow your horn in traffic. This affords total strangers an opportunity to hate you.

6. Park in handicapped parking. This tells the rest of the world that you are shiftless and too lazy to walk a few extra feet.

7. Never go to the movie to see it. Go there to talk.

8. Complain to anyone who will listen, but talk fast because most ain't gonna' wait around to hear your gripes.

9. Hate your job and let everyone know it. This will assure frustration and failure.

10. Be negative. This will reap undreamed of results. Not only will it cause everyone around you to be negative, but it will assure you of someday being buried in an unmarked grave.

Robbie Nell Bell Finds Best Route to Free Beer Is a Dog

Last Saturday at the Possum Hollow Country Fair, I was seated at a table next to the Stephanie Lord Benefit Booth, along with my good friend Bill Adams, Stephanie's uncle. The table had on it five stacks of books that we were selling to help Stephanie buy a much needed chair. Numerous churches and clubs were doing likewise by selling donated cakes and cookies.

About midafternoon two pretty young girls, probably sixteen or seventeen, one very tall and the other very short, approached the table and began thumbing through the books while talking to Bill. I heard one of the girls say they were from Cochran, and I heard the other say, "Here! This is the book you need, *The Official Redneck Handbook.*"

"Are you a redneck?" Bill asked her.

"No, I really ain't," she said, "but I'll guar-on-tee ya' I've dated ever' one uv 'em they is in Bleckley County. An' short as I am I have a heckuva' lot o' trouble climbin' in an' out o' them pickups, like that'n on the' cover o' th' book."

Bill almost fell out of his Dudley Baptist folding chair, and I almost joined him.

I autographed a copy of the book, handed it to the short girl, dropped $5.95 in Stephanie's cigar box, and said to Bill, "You can bet your snuff can *that's* gonna' be in print next week!"

I also saw my old buddy Robbie Nell Bell, from Alma (Robbie Nail Bail, fum Almer) at Possum Hollow. She looks great and, as always, was happy as a lark. And, as always, nothing she says surprises me. Like when she told me about her new dog as we stood and ate pigskins while listening to Al Haywood and Kelly Knight sing.

"Yeah, I had 'im 'baout a month, I reckon," she said. "I bin doin' lots o' travelin' lately in my new job an' Mayel give 'im to me f'r compny an' perteckshun. You 'member Mayel dontcha'?"

"You mean Mel, the fellow who owns Mel's Juke down in Broxton?"

"Yeah, wail, it ain't right in tayoun. It's 'baout a six-pack nawth o'Broxton an'—"

"Right, I remember now. But what about your dog? What kind is it?"

"Oh, he's one o' them highfalutin' dogs. Mayel said he got 'im fum some Yankee headin' saouth who had three uv 'em. He's done bin nockulated n' wormed an' ever'thing. Even had a 'stemper shot."

"Well, is he a cocker spaniel, a bulldog, a poodle, or what?"

"Naw, none o' them. Lemmee see, whut *did* Mayel say he wuz? Hmmmmm . . . Oh yeah! I 'member now. Mayel said he wuz a labbadoor treever. Tha's whut he is. Ya' know anything 'baout labbadoor treevers, newspaper man?"

"Well, I think so. But you mean Labrador retriever, don't you, Robbie Nell?"

"Right, tha's whut I said—labbadoor treever."

"Yeah, right—labbadoor treever," I said with a sigh of resignation and surrender, a sigh I've given many times in the six years I've known Robbie Nell. "By the way, what's his name?"

"Michelob," she said without batting either of her pretty eyes.

"Michelob?" I asked in disbelief.

"Right, Michelob."

"Now tell me, how in the world did you ever come up with a name like that for a dog?"

"I jus' figgered it wuz a good idy, an' it wuz, 'cause it

works," she said as she reached deep in my paper bag for another pigskin.

"It works? What do you mean? What works?"

"Wail, ya' see, newspaper man, it's like this here. I do a whole bunch o'travelin' an' I go in lots o'bars and jukes all over Jawga. But I don't go in no place where I can't take Michelob. An' ever' time I holler at 'im I end up with five or six free beers. I jus' holler 'Michelob!' an' five or six guys bus' their tail t'buy me a beer."

"That really works, Robbie Nell?"

"Dang right! Shoot, I ain't bought a beer since Mayel gimmee th' dawg. Naow I'm thinkin' 'baout gittin' me a nuther'n an' namin' him Jukebox," she said as she winked and poked me in the ribs with her elbow. "Whadda' ya' think o' that?"

"Yeah, I get the picture. You just go in a bar and holler 'Michelob' and 'Jukebox' all night long and sit there and drink beer and listen to country music."

"Ya' got it, newspaper man. Know where I kin git me a 'nuther labbadoor treever?"

"No, not right off hand. But I know a woman who has a cute little German schnauzer she'll give you."

"Come on, newspaper man. Quit pullin' my laig. I don't need no gun, whut I need is a 'nuther dawg."

I made no attempt to explain as I watched my favorite girl down my last pigskin.

Dining with Friends Can Be Quite Unusual

Dining out with friends is, in most cases, a pleasant experience. You know, good conversation, good food, quiet mood music, a laugh or two. That's the way it is in most cases. Sometimes, however, it doesn't quite work out that way.

Like last Friday night when I joined my friend Robbie Nell Bell from Alma (Robbie Nail Bail, fum Almer) and a few of her friends who were helping her celebrate her final decree and permanent separation from Urel Simpson (U-

Rail Seeumpson) from just north of Broxton, based on
"irreconcilable differences."

Having dinner (supper) with Robbie Nail is like dancing
with a giraffe—it'll keep a fella on his toes. And remember
this, Robbie Nail is *always* in charge. I had dinner (supper)
with her and a few of her friends Friday night. I arrived at
the Vidalyur restaurant early, took a seat and waited, but
not for long.

About 7:25 P.M., it sounded like Merrill's Marauders coming in the front door. "We're heeeerrre!" Robbie Nell
shouted in a voice that blew out four candles on a birthday
cake and started a baby to crying. Then she spotted me,
"Hey there, newspaper man! C'mere an' meet my freein's."

"Hello, Robbie Nell," I mumbled. "Good to see you."

"Likewise," she mouthed methodically as she switched
her beer to her left hand and shook. "Glad ya' made it. This
here's Bubba an' T'reessa, fum daown close t' Broxton. An'
this here's Roy Lee an' Ceeundy, fum Wes' Green. An' ya'
already know ol' Mayel who runs the juke where I work,
don'cha?"

"Sure do," I said as I shook hands all around.

"Oh, an' this here's Seeulvya. She works th' night shift at
Mayel's, an' th' day shift, too, whenever I git drunk an'
don't make it in," Robbie Nell explained. "By th' way, you
plannin' t' work t'morrow, ain'tcha?"

"Oh yeah. I done tol' Mama to plan on keepin' th'
young'uns. I been out with ya'b'fore, Robbie Nail," she
said.

"You got that right. Well, le's git on with it. Where 'baouts
y'ont us t' set at, ma'am?"

"I have a table set up for you in the back, next to the
wall," the hostess said.

"Le's git on with it then."

After much maneuvering and compromising as to who
would sit where, we all sat. I landed between Robbie Nail
and Seeulvya. I searched diligently for my safety belt.
Negative.

Shortly, a waitress arrived. "Hi, I'm Brenda and I'll be
your waitress tonight."

"Pleesdtameetcha', Breeunder," Robbie Nail said. "We're hungrier'n a Alabama hobo an' dry's gunpowder. Kin ya' do som'thin 'baout that?"

"Sure can. Would you folks like a drink before you eat?"

"Ya' better bleeve it, Honey. We want us a drink 'fore we eat, atter we eat, an' 'cause we eat. We're in a celebratin' mood t'nite. Jus' brang us 'baout three six-packs o' Bud t' git us started," Robbie Nail commanded. "An' lemme' tell ya' now. Jus' put ever'thang on one check an' give it t' ol' Mayel there, th' one with th' silly lookin' grin on his face. Right, Mayel?"

"Whutever ya' say, Robbie Nail. It's yore party, an' 'sides, it ain't ever day a fella's head waitress jumps off'n th' marriage boat," Mel allowed.

"OK, be right back with the beer," Brenda said.

I uttered a little silent prayer for Brenda. So young, so unsuspecting, so in for the shock of her waitress life. You know, the lamb to the wolves, and all that.

The three six-packs arrived, followed by two more, and then Brenda was ready to take our order.

"Our specials tonight are oysters Rockefeller, served on a bed of spinach, and Alaskan king crablegs," she recited computer-like.

The beer was already taking its toll, and Robbie Nell, as always, was in charge. "Wail, I tail ya', Breeunder. Ol' Rockyfeller c'n have his orsters, give the spinach back to Popeye, and tho' them crablegs in th' dumpster. We all want that big ol' T-bone steak'n fries, right?"

There were no dissenters, myself included. Bubba, Roy Lee, and Mel ordered theirs well done. I went with medium, and all the girls except Sylvia sided with me.

"An' brang us 'baout a number three washtub full o' them onion rangs—Vidalyur onion rangs," Robbie Nell barked. "With this bunch it don't matter none if'n y'r breath stinks. Oh, yeah, 'nother thang—brang us a bunch o' ketch-up, an' 'baout three more six-packs when ya' brang them steaks 'cause we got a heckuva' lot o' celebratin' to do t'night, I guar-On-tee ya'."

By n'by, Brenda brought the steaks, along with gallons of

catsup and more beer. Roy Lee took one look at his T-bone
and whistled Brenda back to our table.

"This'n needs a little more fire, ma'am," he said.

"You mean you'd like it cooked some more?"

"Yessum, that or brang me a piece o' rope. Heck, I got
cows to home whut's been hurt worse'n this'n an' got up an'
run off."

And it was like that as long as I sat there. I got up to leave
about 9:15 P.M. Robbie Nail took exception to that.

"Where 'baouts ya' goin'? Ain't we gonna' shoot no
eight-ball?" she asked.

"No, 'fraid not. Better get on home," I told her. "Thanks
for the steak, Mel. And Robbie Nell, I just hope this divorce
is what you really want, and that things work out for you up
in Nashville. Good luck."

"Thanks, newspaper man. Ever'thing's gonna' be fine,
jus' fine."

"Well, I hope so. Just remember this, marriage is made in
heaven, you know," I said.

"Yeah, and you 'member this," she countered, "so's
thunder an' lightnin'."

Robbie Nell Bell, she may be a redneck, but nobody ever
said she was stupid.

Part 6

Singles in a World of Doubles

It ain't easy, friend. After all, what do you do with leftover Vienna sausage and grits? And what do you do with milk that's turned green and won't pour?

I've been a single in a world of doubles for seventeen glorious years now, and people keep telling me that I just *ought* to be married. One lady told me recently that *everybody* ought to be married. I disagreed, saying to her that it is no more true that everybody *ought* to be married than that everybody *ought* to eat liver.

I have a friend who explains that his divorce ten years ago was very agreeable and amicable. "Not one problem. We split everything 50/50—even the house," he said.

"But Jack, how do you split a house 50/50?" I questioned.

"Simple," he said. "She got the inside, and I got the outside."

The foremost problem that I experience comes with the matchmakers. They can't stand to see a single person happy. Each one has a sister that "You just must meet."

"And why should I meet your sister?" I ask.

"Because she's so lovely and nice, and besides, her fourth husband just passed away last year," I was told. "Any questions?"

"Well, yeah . . . just one," I said.

"And what is that?"

"Just what did them four husbands die from?"

And the story is legend in these parts about the fellow who was on death row, scheduled to be executed the next morning for the death of three wives. The preacher came to visit on his final night and asked, "Now then, John, is there anything you'd like to tell me before your fateful date with the electric chair tomorrow morning?"

"Like what?" John asked.

"Well, maybe like how your three wives died," the preacher urged.

"The fust 'un died fum eatin' rat poison," John said.

"And the second?"

"She died fum eatin' rat poison, too."

"I see," said the preacher. "And what about the third?"

"I blowed her head off with a .12 gauge shotgun," John admitted matter-of-factly, with no sign of remorse.

"Why, John? Why?"

"Cuz she wudn't eat th' rat poison."

It ain't really that bad in the single lane—and to tell you the truth, it ain't all that good, either.

The Pros and Cons of Living Alone

I was strolling through a mall a couple of weeks ago and encountered a lone soul who has recently embarked on the single life via the divorce route. I didn't understand it, but I didn't question it. Question it? Heck, this day and time I wouldn't blink an eye if told that Roy Rogers and Dale Evans had split. Only, "Who gets Trigger?"

She showed me a list of living alone facts she had received from a friend. I got quite a kick out of 'em and, being an expert on the subject, added a few of my own. Do you other singles relate to any of 'em?

The Nice Things about Living Alone
- You can start squeezing a new tube of toothpaste any-place you want to.
- You can take an afternoon nap without feeling guilty.

- You can read a whodunit without anyone telling you who done it.
- You can stack up twenty dollars worth of return-for-deposit bottles and nobody bugs you about it.
- You can make popcorn with your electric blanket.
- You don't have to own a bathrobe.
- You can always leave the bathroom door open.
- You don't have to change bed linens unless you have company coming.
- You don't have to race anyone for the Sunday papers.
- You can mix daiquiris in the washing machine.
- You never have to wait to use the telephone and it's never busy when you call home.
- When you open a can of mixed nuts you can eat *all* the cashews.
- You can heat your coffee roll with your hair dryer.
- Free samples that come addressed to Occupant are all yours.
- You can put your cigarette butt anyplace you like.
- There's no one to pick up after you and, better yet, no one to remind you they picked up after you.
- You can answer a midnight phone call, or make one, and not have to explain it.
- When you burp, you don't have to say "excuse me" to yourself.
- There's no wait to get in the bathroom in the morning.
- You can wash one dish at a time—as you need it.
- You don't have to hide magazines.
- You can cut the grass when *you're* ready.
- You can sing as loud as you please in the shower and there's no one to laugh at you.
- You can eat potato chips and crackers in bed without anybody glaring at you.
- You can run around the house with a half-pound of white cream on your face and no one calls you Marcel Marceau.
- You can drink orange juice right out of the bottle.
- You can park smack in the middle of a two-car garage.
- You can leave the stereo and all that rock junk turned off for months at a time.

The Tough Things about Living Alone

- There's nobody to sit on your feet when you do sit-ups.
- If you get caught in a zipper, you stay caught.
- You're always the first to know when you're out of toilet paper.
- There's nobody around to hand you a towel when you shampoo and get soap in your eyes.
- When you have a nightmare, there's no one around to wake you until it's over.
- When the late, late show is on you have to watch *Psycho* all by yourself—and then shower.
- The toilet seat is hardly ever warm.
- All the jokes you tell yourself, you've heard before.
- If you forget your house key, there's no one to wake up to let you in.
- On your birthday all you can do is yell "Happy Birthday!" down the kitchen sink drain and listen to the echo.
- When you go on a diet, there's no one to tell you you look thinner. So, you lie to yourself.
- You talk to yourself and, even worse, you're the only one around to listen.
- It's impossible to defrost half a pizza or open half a can of soup.
- If your dress zips up the back, you have to put it on frontwards and jump around fast.
- There's no one to hold down the string when you wrap a package.
- You have to put away Christmas decorations all by yourself.
- When your bank account is overdrawn (or underdeposited) you know who done it.
- You always have to sniff the milk before you drink it.
- The telephone always rings when you're in the tub.
- You have to clean up your own mess after cooking fish.

So there they are, the pros and cons of living alone. Which outweighs the other? Take your pick. And, should you feel lonely and want someone to talk to? You can always go to the laundromat.

Batchin' It on Television Was a Ball

Do you watch TV very much? I remember the days when I
was addicted to the point where about the only sounds in
the Whaley household were, "Shhhhh!" "Switch channels,"
and "Where's the *TV Guide*?" I watched everything from
Captain Kangaroo to Tarzan and wore out a La-Z-Boy recliner every other year. Each morning I'd exchange the
same dialogue with my secretary.

"God, your eyes look awful, Mr. Whaley!" she'd say.

"Yeah? Well, you oughta' see 'em from my side, Peggy,"
I'd tell her.

I took the cure in '73. *Reader's Digest* replaced the *TV
Guide*. Montavanni and Mancini replaced Captain Kangaroo and Tarzan. A Panasonic stereo took the place of my
Quasar, a happy divorce. And my eyes cleared up, both
sides.

During my twenty-year addiction I found TV bachelors
interesting, especially the private detectives. Man, they led
exciting and romantic lives! Remember?

I'd sit in my La-Z-Boy munching potato chips and dip or
cheese and crackers wearing my skivvies and runover-at-
the-heel slippers. On TV, Mr. Everything breezed along the
beach at Malibu with Venus curled up in the seat beside
him. Periodically, she'd flash that "I'm all yours, baby,"
smile as he maneuvered his Mercedes or Porsche over the
ocean road. You know where they were headed, don't you?
Either to board his yacht and sail away to his private island
or to his beach house high above the roaring Pacific for fun
and games.

I remember other things about those TV bachelors, too.
They never waited for change. Remember? After he and
Venus finished their drinks in the swankiest bar in California or New York, he'd take a roll from his pocket that would
clog the Lake Sinclair flood gates. He'd drop a bill or two
on the checkered tablecloth, flip a few in the direction of the
bartender, and slip a couple more to the guy who brought
his sports car to the entrance. No change! The guy never
waited for change, possibly explaining why he never had

any in the first place. I never saw a TV bachelor pay for anything with the correct change.

Parking spaces? Always! He'd maneuver that sports baby snakelike in Manhattan to Forty-second and Broadway, zip to the curb, park, and walk away. Ever been to Manhattan? Baby, there ain't room to park a skateboard at Forty-second and Broadway!

I also remember the monograms. Everything he owned was monogrammed: car door, pajamas, briefcase, shirts, handkerchiefs, toilet tissue, stationery. You name it. The everpresent BW was there.

And those TV bachelor apartments! Dreamland, right? Flip a switch, and mood music invaded every nook and cranny. A bar and a pool were standard items; no TV bachelor would dream of going home without one. Ice was always in a container on the bar and the refrigerator bulged with goodies from an expensive delicatessen. A velour sofa surrounded a giant coffee table and there were more pillows than you could shake a martini at. Carpet? Up to your kneecaps, baby! Fireplace? What a silly question!

Bright sunshine always flitted through the kitchen window by day, while moonlight or soft rain danced a minuet on the ledge outside the bay window at night. Always just enough light to make me curious when he and Venus stood silhouetted in front of the open window. And, the music played on . . .

Then, There's the Real Bachelor World

I was sitting in my kitchen (?) a couple of Saturday nights ago clad in my un-monogrammed skivvies and runover-at-the-heels slippers when the phone rang. It was early, about 7:30. I walked to the den where my TV would be, if I owned one, and answered.

"Hello?"

"Hey, Bo! Whatcha' doin', gettin' ready to hit the town?" my friend asked.

I played it straight.

"Naw, just sittin' here sortin' socks," I told him.

"You're doin' what?" he asked.

"Sortin' socks," I repeated matter-of-factly, just like everybody in Dublin sorts socks every Saturday night about 7:30.

"Man, Saturday night ain't no time to be doin' laundry! Come on and let's—"

"I ain't doin' laundry. I'm sortin' socks and—"

"Well, heck, you had to wash 'em first, right?"

"Right. I washed 'em in May. Just ain't sorted 'em yet. I always put it off long as I can 'cause I'm color blind and—"

"Color blind? Aw, come on! You puttin' me on?" he asked.

"Nope, that's a fact," I told him.

"Man, what colors you have trouble with?"

"Well, the blacks and whites don't bother me. Other than those, it's a wipe out."

"Well, I'll be doggone! Color blind . . . Whatcha' gonna' do after you finish with the socks?"

"Fold T-shirts."

"Sounds like fun. Need any help?" he asked.

"Oh, I don't think so. I don't have any problem with T-shirts.

"Why not?"

"They're all white," I told him.

"Yeah, well, have fun. See you later. We'll all be over at Fred's if you wanna' come later."

"Thanks, I'll probably stay here. What the heck, I may just shine shoes! And, I have some shirts I washed July fourth that need hanging up . . ."

It's Time to Stop Discrimination against Singles

I have never been one to climb up on the proverbial soap box and wail the injustices of discrimination, but I'm fed up with some forms of it. For fifteen years I've swallowed blatant discrimination against us single folks, but remained silent. No more! What society does to us is a shame, and I'm ready to speak out.

What prompted this sudden turnaround of a meek, even-tempered, and subdued introvert like me to a raging, fire-spitting, tempestuous dragon with revenge in his eyes and the wrath of a scorned woman on his tongue? Two things: I cleaned out my refrigerator and made my annual trek to the supermarket last Saturday.

Is there a single out there in the hinterlands who's cleaned out the refrigerator lately? I'll tell you, it can be a revelation.

I almost gave up when I opened the refrigerator door because Saturday morning is no time to view the remains of half a boiled ham and three cartons of solid milk. The ham was all crinkly and dark brown around the edges. The milk? Well, that's what really set off my tantrum regarding discrimination against us singles.

The dairies imprint a date on the top of the milk carton. I appreciate that, but why the heck don't they go the second mile for us singles and complete the job?

My three milk cartons bore these dates: February 17, June 10, and September 9. But no year! What good does it do a single to know the month and day without the year? Discrimination, that's what it is.

I'm convinced that the milk in one of my cartons came from Mrs. O'Leary's cow, the one that kicked over the lamp that started the Chicago fire October 8, 1871. But I couldn't determine which one without the year, so I had no choice but to throw all three out.

I then tackled the five partial loaves of bread, and a few fishes. You think they have hard bread in New Jersey delicatessens? Three of mine could have been used as a blacksmith's anvil. And speaking of bread, why don't the bakeries take us singles into consideration and package half a loaf?

And what do you do with four Vidalia onions purchased in 1979? Well, if you're single you take a big screwdriver and do your dead level best to loosen them from the bottom of the drawer in the little compartment marked "Produce." You think Vidalia onions are white? Negative. My four were as black as charcoal briquettes, and as hard as I tried I couldn't keep them lit—no matter how much starter I used.

Cheese won't keep forever either; neither will salami. I

threw out two packages of Hickory Farms cheese that had more mold than the mushrooms at the CAMSCO mushroom farm, and about four inches of salami that looked like the three two-month-old bananas I threw away at the same time.

It almost broke my heart to have to do away with a slice of my mother's birthday cake, especially since my daughter baked it—last June.

Next, I deposited nine black olives in the garbage can. The fact that they were nine green olives when I placed them in the refrigerator last Christmas is really of no significance. I'll tell you, food just won't keep like it used to.

I also threw out a huge hanging basket, although it was an Irish potato when it joined the olives on New Year's Day.

The only thing I salvaged was a pair of vice-grip pliers. They were behind a Kentucky Fried Chicken box, partially filled with mashed potatoes and two wings. The box came from my friend, Elbert Mullis, during the St. Patrick's Festival—in 1980.

How did the pliers get in there? I vaguely recall using them to change the light bulb after my orange juice exploded and demolished it in 1980.

Finally, I found it necessary to throw out three beautiful Georgia peaches, Linda, Margo, and Cindy, because I just flat don't like females around poking fun when I renovate my refrigerator.

Now then, if I can just find my kitchen sink, I'll renovate it, too. I vaguely recall that the last time I saw it, it was flanked by a Mr. Coffee on the left and an electric can opener on the right.

And, if I can't find it I'll listen for it because the faucet drips twenty-four hours a day. If it ever stops I won't be able to sleep a wink.

I'll be like the old gentleman who lived next to a municipal airport for thirty years, with big jets taking off every minute and flying directly over his house. Then, the city built a new airport and closed the old one, with the final take-off at midnight of the last day it was in operation.

The old gentleman, sound asleep, sat up in bed at 12:05

A.M. and shouted at the top of his voice, "My God! What was that quiet?"

It's Not All a Matter of Record

Every Saturday morning, I follow the same routine: throw a shoe at the alarm clock, try to find the floor, and stare at the apparition in the bathroom mirror, Igor, the Hunchback of Notre Dame.

Satisfied that I am still a resident of this world, I head for a restaurant, breakfast and gallons of plasma. Plus the morning newspapers, a must.

What do I read? Everything! And that includes "From the Record," which contains, among other things, who's getting married and who's getting divorced. Do you have any idea how many of each happen during the course of a year? Take a look. The figures came from the probate court (marriages) and clerk of the courts (divorces) for the past twelve months: 400 marriages and 289 divorces.

Statistics are cold, aren't they? They only tell part of the story. No way can they portray the concerns and heartaches of the 578 who called it quits, or the bliss, hopes, and expectations of the 800 who said, "I do."

I was only interested in numbers, no names.

Being somewhat experienced in the divorce field, I've devised a list of ten ways to identify those who've "cut the dinghy loose," as they say. I'm sure you have others.

Women

1. They buy their jeans one size smaller and wear a big turquoise ring on their left hand.

2. They add at least four more gold chains to the six already hanging around their neck.

3. They pump their own gas.

4. They enroll in night classes and read the classified ads.

5. They're on a crash diet to lose fifteen pounds and four inches.

6. They go where the crowd is.

7. They smile a lot (on the outside) and cry a lot (on the inside).

8. They eat a lot of yogurt and skip a lot of meals.

9. Dear Abby becomes their personal counselor.

10. They lie a lot, making statements such as, "Never again! I'm through with men! They're all alike. I'm happier than I've ever been in life. I really enjoy just staying home and watching TV."

Men

1. In the supermarket, they're usually found in the TV dinner and Vienna sausage aisles.

2. The Sunday morning papers that used to be in the house by 8:00 A.M. are still on the front lawn at 11:15.

3. He grows a beard or a moustache, or both, and unbuttons his shirt down to his bellybutton.

4. He's traded his sedan for a sports car or a Jeep.

5. He's a regular at the laundromat on Saturday mornings (late).

6. On Sunday morning he wears a wrinkled shirt.

7. On Monday morning he wears a slightly dirty wrinkled shirt, with two buttons missing.

8. He'll have a telltale white circle on his ring finger, left hand.

9. He becomes well acquainted with the restaurant crowd and is on a first-name basis with the waitresses.

10. He visits his mother more often.

Part 7

Love, Marriage, and Family

I don't believe there has ever been a book written that didn't have a section in it that was closer to the author's heart than the others. This one is mine, and I don't want to mess with it here. It means too much to me, especially the people involved in the stories. They are so special to me.

Please forgive my brevity in introducing them to you. I love 'em, and I hope you will when you finish this section.

Romance with a Can of WD–40 in Hand

Several months ago I had lunch in Macon with two of that city's loveliest young ladies. I'll call them Lisa and Deedee. They're best friends. This chapter is about Deedee and her husband, whom I'll call Tommy.

Deedee is beautiful, but then so is Lisa. You know Deedee has to be beautiful when even the *girls* in the office talk about how beautiful she is. And she has a great sense of humor, as you will learn from the following story she told, which she swears is true:

It was a cold and rainy Saturday afternoon last January as Deedee waited for Tommy to get home from his auto parts store. He wasn't due for three hours. As she watched the

149

rain falling, she conjured up a plan, a romantic plan, straight from a Hollywood scriptwriter's pen. She quickly went into action.

First, a roaring fire in the fireplace. Then to the store for steaks. Next, to the video rental for a romantic movie and to a lingerie shop for a short nightgown, black with lots of lace and *very* sheer. And a final stop at a package shop for champagne.

"I want whichever one has the highest octane," she told the clerk.

Back home, she put the steaks and champagne in the refrigerator, added a log to the fire, and spread a quilt and *one* pillow on the floor in front of the fireplace. She then took a shower, eased into her new nightie, put on her makeup, and "did" her hair.

Business was slow, so Tommy was twenty minutes early. He kissed Deedee and showered, shaved, and eased into his pajamas before sitting down to a great steak dinner, complete with candlelight, champagne, and a Barbara Streisand tape just loud enough to be effective.

After dinner they retired to the den, Deedee hugging the champagne and two wine glasses. They reclined on the quilt and *one* pillow to watch the 1960 Academy Award winner *The Apartment*. Deedee was pouring and knew the high octane fuel was working when Tommy eased an arm around her, pulled her gently to him, and kissed her. She poured more champagne, smiled a knowing smile, and shared the lone pillow.

But, the best laid plans of mice and men (and women). . .

When the movie ended Deedee went to brush her teeth. That's when *it* happened:

"My teeth are real close together. I ripped off a piece of dental floss about eight inches long so I could get a good hold on it," she explained. "But it stuck between two front teeth. I ripped off another piece to try and get the first piece out. But it stuck, too, and I had doubled my trouble. There I stood, in my short nightie, looking like a werewolf with four four-inch fangs hanging down to my chin. I yelled to Tommy and he came running."

"What happened?" he asked.

"I can't get this darn dental floss from between my teeth," she said.

"I'll be right back!" Tommy said.

"I heard the garage door slam and began crying, afraid he was leaving me. Then I heard the door to his pickup slam and I was sure of it," Deedee said. "But then I heard the garage door open and Tommy appeared at my side."

"Lie on your back."

"I did, with my head in the lavatory and my feet underneath the towel rack."

"Open your mouth, wide!"

"I did and he squirted something between my teeth that tasted awful, but the dental floss came right out easily."

"All through," he said.

"What was that awful tasting stuff you squirted in my mouth, Tommy?"

"WD–40! It works every time."

Is that the end of the story? I'm not sure. I do know that what you just read happened in January and Deedee gave birth to a baby boy in October.

Isn't it amazing what can be accomplished with a bottle of high octane champagne, a beautiful wife with a romantic plan, and a husband who loves her with a can of WD–40 in hand?

I just hope Deedee and Tommy remember that every southern boy needs a nickname or initials. I think W.D. would be about perfect.

Beauty and the Beach

Socrates defined beauty as a short-lived tyranny; Plato called it a privilege of nature; Theocritus, a delightful prejudice.

Sir Francis Bacon wrote, "The best part of beauty is that which no picture can express."

And then, there was Confucius who said, "Everything has its beauty but not everyone sees it."

I wish these scholars could have been with me on a recent visit to Jekyll Island. Some beauty is so infinite that words are inadequate to capture and preserve it. Such was the case at Jekyll Island.

I arose early, very early. The sun had preceded me by just a few minutes and was not yet at full glow as it peeped over the Atlantic. Its rays danced a rumba to the steady beat of roaring waves.

Walking shirtless and barefooted the hundred or so yards to the rim of the ocean, I felt the vastness and infinity of nature. Thousands upon thousands of footprints, large and small, dotted the sandy path, evidence that throngs had trodden the path before me, some going to and some coming from the salty basin.

Once seated on the beach I realized that I was alone. A huge ship dotted the horizon. It was impossible to determine if it was going or coming. Its gigantic dimensions were reduced to microscopic proportions when compared to the impatient Atlantic on which it sailed. And, I listened. Yes, oceans do roar.

Ignoring the vastness of the ocean for the moment, I cast my eyes upward as I sat there in the sand, spent waves teasing my toes. A lone cloud hovered and sauntered about the heavens, carefree and lazy. It was billowy bright, towering, shimmering, and fluffy, like a just-bathed poodle or cotton candy. It fascinated me. And then, it was gone, on to where clouds go, on and on.

Socrates was right. . . .

Deserted by the cloud, I returned my attention to the ocean. It was my turn to tease the spent waves and white-caps with my toes as they tiptoed softly to shore and expired. (One took me seriously and slipped up on me as my attention was diverted back to the sky and another cloud. It attacked and wet my bottom almost as if to say, "Gotcha'.")

I decided to walk along the beach, why I don't know. One mile of beach is like any other mile of beach. However, there's just something about walking on a beach, and it's a good way to dry your britches.

An impatient breeze caressed my face and held my hand.

Alone? I have to think not. The beauties of nature surrounded me. It was good to be alive.

Plato was right, too. . .

Having dined heartily on such delicacies as cotton candy
clouds, salt water whitecaps, and seabreezes, I retraced my
steps in the sand to my motel room to change to dry
britches, don shoes and shirt, and treated myself to Sunday
morning breakfast. With me it isn't a meal, it's a ritual, a
bonus for having survived the night.

Little did I know that I would view the most beautiful
sight on Jekyll Island as I shuffled along to the motel restaurant, stopping en route to purchase what for me is a breakfast must, a newspaper.

Inside the restaurant, the smell of fresh brewed coffee ig-
nited my already gigantic appetite. The anticipation of soft
scrambled eggs, sausage, grits, biscuit, grapefruit, and an
hour or more with my paper provided additional fuel for a
fiery appetite.

I was well into my second cup of coffee and partially
finished with my sausage and eggs, when he came in. Who
is he? He was a giant of a man wearing a black T-shirt with a
motorcycle emblem emblazoned across the chest, a massive chest. His biceps strained for freedom, testing every
stitch. Immediately I recognized two areas of common interest with the man, motorcycles and newspapers. He had
one tucked under his arm as he walked to his table. (What?
A motorcycle or a newspaper, you ask? Friend, the man
could have had one of each. He was that big!)

With a terrific breakfast under my belt, I gave full attention to my newspaper and the remaining half cup of coffee.
Emmaline and Hessie's couldn't have served a more pleasant and tasteful meal, their broiled lobster and crabmeat au
gratin notwithstanding.

From a nearby table I heard the last words of a conversation, an obvious reference to my friend in the motorcycle T-shirt.

"Oh, he's just one of them motorcycle bums."

I was all finished with breakfast and nearing the end of
the final section of my paper when they came in. They? Yes,

a beautiful lady and a little girl, maybe five or six years old. Both were wearing beach outfits and gorgeous suntans. (I had something in common with the child, too. She had a wet bottom. I soon learned that she'd been to my ocean for a prebreakfast swim. I wondered if she might have seen my cloud.) Both lady and child were happy and giggling when they arrived. They already had a table. The lady's husband and the little girl's father was seated at it. Right, the man in the motorcycle T-shirt. You know, "One of them motorcycle bums."

He rose, helped his wife with her chair, and patted the child on her fanny, a privilege reserved for daddies, before lifting her to her chair.

"Have a good swim?" he asked.

"Beautiful! Absolutely beautiful," the wife answered.

The child was as fresh as clean linen and as cute as the little girl in the Coppertone ad, complete with pony tail. The only thing missing was the determined Scottie tugging at her shorts.

I folded my paper and watched. The three of them glowed in the joy of each other's company as they made small talk and the "motorcycle bum" examined in detail a small shell found and prized by his daughter. She gave it to him and he kissed her on the forehead. She giggled. Her mother smiled.

Sir Francis Bacon? Obviously a wise man, and he was right.

Their breakfast arrived, I viewed a beautiful sight.

Obviously, the child was well trained. She knew exactly what to do with her napkin, knife, fork, spoon, *and* hands. Just as naturally as breathing she bowed her head and reached right and left with them. Right to Daddy and left to Mommy. Her pony tail lay as still as a weeping willow on a calm day.

The motorcycle bum? He offered a prayer of thanks for his family and the food before them.

The guy who had labeled the little girl's father "just one of them motorcycle bums" had left. I wished he hadn't. I would have given my breakfast and newspaper for him to have been there.

Confucius? You be the judge.

*   *   *

As for me? I have the feeling that I witnessed the most beautiful sight on Jekyll Island that Sunday morning in a busy motel restaurant.

It's Best to Look Before You Leap

The Sea of Matrimony is an ocean of troubled waters these days. Maybe people don't look long enough before taking the marital leap, so read further before leaping.

Ten Wives to Look Out For

1. "I've finally cured my husband of biting his fingernails," Mrs. Barkum declared. "How?" asked a neighbor. "Simple, I hid his teeth."

2. As they left the party, a wife said to her husband, "Elmer, did anybody tell you tonight that you were ordained to be the life of the party—the greatest raconteur, the greatest wit, the greatest lover boy in town?" "No, dear," Elmer replied. "Nobody did." "Exactly," said the wife grimly. "So answer me this: where the heck did you ever get the idea?"

3. Overheard at a woman's club: "Wouldn't it be nice, Ethel, if marriage licenses expired every five years like driver's licenses?"

4. A wife was picking out a neat, pearl handled, six-shot revolver when her husband ambled into the store. "Oh, don't bother wrapping it," she instructed the clerk. "Here he comes now."

5. A frowning doctor told Mrs. Gumbach, "Frankly, I don't like the looks of your husband." "Well, neither do I—but he *is* good to the children."

6. At the cocktail party, Pete was seen hanging from a tree limb in the back yard by his wife, who approached the hostess and said, "I'm sorry but the time has come to bid you adieu. Pete Henry is doing his imitation of Spanish moss in the back yard."

7. The coroner shot a sympathetic glance at the young

widow dressed in black, with tears streaming down her face. "I'm sorry to have to bother you at a time like this," he said gently, "but can you possibly recall your dead husband's last words?" The sobbing widow dabbed at her tears and replied, "Indeed I can. He said, 'Don't try to scare me with that shotgun. You couldn't hit the broad side of a barn with it.'"

8. It was a cold and cruel wife who told her husband after they arrived home from the party: "Well! You sure made a prize fool of yourself tonight! I'm just thankful the other guests didn't realize you were sober."

9. Mrs. Newton watched in silence as long as she could stand it while her bald and plump middle-aged husband ogled a striking blonde in a skin-tight, low-cut, *very* revealing cocktail dress. Then, she hissed in his ear, "I'll bet her kitchen sink is well stacked, too!"

10. A henpecked husband finally did something on his own—he dropped dead while doing the dishes. His nagging wife mourned her loss and the fact that she had nobody left to badger. A visitor stopped by the day after the funeral and sympathized. "Oh, Gladys, how you must miss dear Wilbur," she said. "Yes," sighed the widow wistfully, "I do. Why it seems but yesterday that he stood at that door, laundry in hand, holding it open until two flies came in."

And Ten Husbands

1. A mousey little man was hauled into court for beating his wife, a mammoth creature. The judge, trying in vain to conceal a certain amount of admiration, demanded, "What came over you?" "Well, Your Honor, it was like this: She had her back to me, the fire poker was handy, and the back door was open. I couldn't resist. So, I took a chance."

2. At a New Year's party, a husband whispered to his wife as she was putting on her coat to leave, "What did I say to annoy you, dear? I'd really like to know because it may come in handy again one day."

3. "My wife," boasted the well-to-do jeweler, "has but one extravagance. She just dearly loves to spend money."

4. A prisoner was reminiscing with a fellow inmate about the fun he and his wife had enjoyed at the beach burying

each other in the sand. "I guess the only proper thing to do when I get out is to go back and dig her up."

5. "I thought I was set for life," said the husband while having a drink with friends at his club. "I had a flourishing business, a healthy bank balance, a beautiful home, and the love of a gorgeous and passionate woman." "Well, what happened?" asked a fellow drinker. "Wham! One night, right out of the blue, my wife walked in!"

6. "You know darn well I have better judgment than you!" a wife screamed at her husband during an argument. "Yes, I agree. You married me—and I married you."

7. An old gaffer told his golfing partner following their daily round, "My wife and I were married fifty-five years ago—and we still hold hands." Then, he added, "We have to. If we didn't, we'd kill each other!"

8. An American psychologist, touring Mexico, wondered why peons always ride on burros while their wives walk behind. Finally, his curiosity got the best of him and he stopped a peasant to ask the reason for such an arrangement. "But, Señor," the peasant replied, "my wife, she don't own a burro."

9. A silver-haired widower in his early eighties had this inscribed on his wife's tombstone in his great hour of bereavement: "My Light Has Gone Out." Within six months he married again, a twenty-five-year-old girl. Feeling some explanation was due the viewers of his first wife's tombstone, he commissioned a granite carver to inscribe these words underneath the original inscription: "I Have Struck Another Match!"

10. Loyalty sometimes proves embarrassing, like in the case of the wife whose commuter husband was unusually late one Friday night. So, she sent identical telegrams to five of his friends: "Jack not home. Stop. Is he spending night with you? Stop. Urgent you reply. Stop. Jean." The unfortunate Jack arrived home shortly afterward, and his arrival was followed by five telegrams—all saying "Yes."

Fantasy of the Perfect Date Is Fulfilled

I doubt that there is a man alive who doesn't harbor fantasies. I do, three in particular: to write the Great American Novel; to become a par golfer; to know the joy of "the perfect date."

I gave up on the first two long ago, and until recently had all but given up on the third. But I now know the joy of having had "the perfect date."

It began when I visited a Macon office last May 26 and saw the most beautiful girl I'd ever seen. She was tall, blonde, well-dressed, bronzed from the beach sun, and flashed a contagious smile.

I invited her to join me for lunch and she accepted! After lunch we walked back to her office where I bid her farewell, but not before learning that it was her twenty-fifth birthday. Later that day I sent her a dozen roses.

Now then, about the perfect date, the perfect evening. It happened on a recent long weekend. I had no plans other than to do my laundry and found myself longing to have dinner with a pretty girl, so I called my young friend and invited her to join me. Again, she accepted!

"You make the reservations and I'll pick you up at seven," I told her.

"All right," she agreed, "see you at seven."

I showered, shaved and dressed, whistling as I did so. And I almost drowned myself in after-shave lotion before driving to Macon and an apartment on Twin Pines Drive.

She was ready, waiting, and gorgeous—dressed in a bright red blouse, a tan striped skirt, and high heels—and groomed to perfection She smelled even better than I did.

"Hi!" she called from the doorway. "I made reservations for 7:30, O.K.?"

"Fine," I said. "Should we go now?"

"I think so. Want me to drive? The place is a little out of the way," she explained.

"Be my guest," I said, handing her the car keys.

We arrived right on time. The hostess seated us at a corner table and lit the candle. Shortly, the waiter brought the traditional white wine and we raised our glasses, touched them together lightly, and I proposed a toast, "to you, honey."

The candle flickered, the wine sparkled, her eyes danced, and my heart swelled as soft music invaded our table. I sipped the wine and feasted on the beauty of my date, fully aware that other diners were eyeing us with obvious curiosity—and me with envy. I could read their lips:

"What in the world is she doing with that old man?"

"Boy! He must be loaded!"

"Lord! What some girls won't do these days for a free meal."

As we dined on filet mignon and prime rib, the conversation flowed as gently as sweet Afton and I learned that she grew up in Swainsboro. Also, that she is well acquainted with my son, Joe. I was as proud as a peacock to be with her.

After dinner, we drove back to her apartment and she invited me in. I accepted, naturally.

"Let me take your coat," she said. "Just make yourself at home while I go to the bedroom and slip into something more comfortable."

I relaxed in a recliner, closed my eyes, and waited. Soon, she reappeared wearing a full-length white terry cloth robe. Her long blond hair fell loosely halfway down her back when she "shook it loose and let it fall." She moved to the stereo and inserted a Nat King Cole tape before moving to the sofa, sitting down, and tucking her long legs under her as girls are prone to do. Then, she turned the table lamp down two notches to complement the song that Mr. Cole was singing, "This Is a Lovely Way to Spend an Evening." Amen!

"You look tired," she said, patting her lap. "Here, let me loosen your tie and you put your head here in my lap and let me help you relax."

I willingly did her bidding and she proceeded to gently massage my neck just below the ears with her long, soft fingers. Then the temples and the forehead. A man just can't buy the feeling such attention produces.

"Feel good?" she asked.

"Ummmmmm . . ." was all I could muster.

"I think you'll be asleep in five minutes," she allowed. "You're welcome to spend the night here with me if you'd like."

It was tempting, oh so tempting . . .

"Thanks, I appreciate it, but I'd better get on to Dublin," I told her.

"Well, maybe another night, O.K.?"

"Right, another night . . ."

It was nearing midnight as we moved to the front porch. I looked at her there in the moonlight, more beautiful than ever. I looked at the stars—and counted my lucky ones. I was nearing the end of a perfect evening. Beautiful, but short. Much too short.

And, yes, there was the time-honored goodnight kiss.

"You be real careful driving home, O.K.?" she cautioned as she squeezed my hand. "And call me when you get there. Promise?"

"Right. I promise."

"And thanks for the dinner. It was a beautiful evening. Come back whenever you like," she said, flashing her All-American smile.

"Thank you, honey. It was a perfect evening," I said before walking to my car.

I stopped for one last look before opening the car door. There she stood, beautiful and genuine. No pretenses. But more than that—I knew she loved me. And believe me, that's the most important ingredient in a perfect date.

"Goodnight, Lisa!" I called back to her.

"Goodnight, Daddy!"

. . . Then I drove back home. My third fantasy had been fulfilled completely.

Next-door Daughter Can Alter Routine in a Hurry

Certain events in life can alter a person's daily routine dramatically. I'm fast learning that to be a fact. You see, my daughter Lisa moved in next door to me one September and then Christmas brought an addition to the Whaley compound on North Elm Street. Santa Claus left a little Pekingese, Chen, at her house Christmas morning.

Prior to September, or B. L. (Before Lisa), my days more or less followed the same routine: get up, shower and shave, a cup of coffee, amble on over to WMLT to meet Bucky and do our morning "Bo and Bucky" show from 7:30 to 8:30, downtown for another cup and fellowship, back to WMLT for my 9:30 to 10:00 radio show, "Music in the Morning," and then head for *The Courier Herald* and my trusty typewriter. Not so any more. Now it's like I was married again, God forbid! Lisa has more errands for me to do than I can list on a legal pad.

She heads out for Macon and her job at Charter Medical every morning around 7:30 A.M. but leaves me assignments in the form of notes on my front door to be done before she returns home about 7 P.M. Also, if she thinks of more errands for me to run during the day, she calls and leaves them on my telephone answering machine. Here's an example. I received this message, in poetic(?) form no less, on a memorable Friday afternoon:

Daddy, this is your daughter—and I don't mean to be rude; but if you don't pick up my dry cleaning, I'll have to go to work in the nude.

O.K., I did as told. I hightailed it on down to Superior Laundry and picked up her dry cleaning. Of course, I figured she should be advised that I had done it, even though I was six days late doing it. So I called a friend of hers, Lisa Coleman, who works in the same office, and left this message for my daughter:

Lisa, my dear, your dry cleaning will be home upon your arrival; but in the future, you can dress for work like Lady Godiva! You see, I know you are neat and I know you are thrifty; but the cost of your dry cleaning comes to $18.50!

Then, there was the morning recently when I found this

little gem hanging on my door when I returned home from
the radio station:

*Daddy, my car wouldn't crank, and I'm running behind:
Please get mine fixed, if you don't mind. Be home about
seven, or seven-thirty; and you might have the oil
changed—10W-30.*

Did I do as ordered? Sure I did. Did I answer her note?
Sure I did. I left it on the front seat of her car:

*My Darling Daughter, I found your note, your car's run-
ning again. Had it jumped off, but it cost me ten. So a word
of advice—let me tell you right off. The next time you park
it, turn the dash light off!*

You would think that with her dry cleaning hanging in her
closet and her car running again, I would be able to get back
on routine. No way, Hosea. What I've related is all B.C.
(Before Chen).

The arrival of the puppy next door simply prompted an
addition to my list of chores as Lisa's handyman. Like her
first day at work after the Christmas holidays when this
message found its way to my answering machine:

*Hello, Puppysitter, this is Lisa. Take my puppy out, will
ya' please, sir? His food's in the cabinet, and give him some
water. Thanks, I 'preciate it, Your next-door Daughter.*

This, of course, prompted another call to the Charter
Medical office building in Macon—and another reply to her
message:

*This is your daddy, and your puppy's getting better; but
tell me this, is he a pointer or a setter? Your grass is well
sprinkled, he missed not a blade; he piddled in the sunshine, as well as in the shade. And one thing for sure, I can
tell you now; I'm glad Santa left you a puppy, instead of a
cow!"*

What Do You Do with Grandchildren?

"Know what a father is?"

"Well, he's a man whose daughter marries a man vastly her inferior, mentally, but then gives birth to unbelievably brilliant grandchildren."

I'm into the grandpa bit, having a grandson who recently turned three. Did I go to see him? Yes, and as always, the visit was too short.

I watched his daddy build a ship from little plastic pieces while the boy lay prone on the floor, watching, chin in hand. (Why is the camera never around when you need it?) The ship had the tallest smoke stack I ever saw. Looked like an egg carton with the Empire State Building stuck in it. All 102 stories.

Next, my turn.

"You make one, Granddaddy Bo," he said, handing me a double handful of red, white, and blue plastic pieces with holes in 'em.

Build a better mousetrap? Nope. Build a higher smoke stack? I did. The Empire State Building now has 103 stories and is 1,250 feet, one inch high.

What do you do with grandchildren? You play with them. Sometimes they'll nearly kill you; but you play with them. You forget your age and go ahead. You'll remember it next morning.

On my way home I thought about 'em, grandparents and grandchildren. We let the little rascals do things to us that start fights otherwise. For example:

You lift him up and sit him on your lap. He giggles and slobbers and you grin and wipe. It's called one-on-one. The world has stopped for a few moments. No one else exists.

Suddenly, and with the quickness of a snake's fang, he rips off your bifocals and slings them across the room! They bounce off the TV and land in the magazine rack.

Do you become violently angry, scold him, and banish him to his room? I think not, Gramps. More than likely you will say something like:

"Hey, Mama! Did you see that?

"He threw those glasses all the way across the room, and, left-handed! The kid's gonna be O.K. Must be thirty feet or more across this room. Looks like you gotcha' a pitcher or a first baseman, Son."

Next, it's Grandma's turn.

She spent two hours and sixty-five dollars at the beauty shop the day before the grandchildren, ages two and four months, arrived. Every hair in place and colored (rinsed). Let it drizzle and she'll cover up like a turtle.

Her new dress complements her hairdo as she sits with Grandpa in their favorite restaurant the night before the grandchildren are to arrive.

Wanna' see a mad Grandma? Just let the waitress brush past her and upset one curl or spill just one drop of milk on the shoulder of her new Jonathan Logan. Does she burn? Makes the microwave in the kitchen look like a refrigerator.

But next day she'll feed that baby, let him pull every curl out, then lay his head on her shoulder. Jonathan Logan be damned. Then, she'll walk and pat, and wait. And wait.

Finally, here it comes! "Buuuuurrrppp!" Similac covers the right shoulder of a drowning Jonathan Logan. Is Grandma mad? Never!

"Didya' hear that? How about that? I'll bet he's never burped like that before, huh?" she brags.

Enter the daughter.

"Oh, Mama! I'm sorry. All over your new dress and—"

"Bah! Who cares? Didya' hear him, Dianne? Hear him burp? Bet he never burped like that for you, huh. Wow! I'll tell ya' he's just—"

"Buuuurrrppp!"

"See there! Isn't he something!"

Grandpa can't stand it.

"Here, let me have him while you get cleaned up. I'll just sit here and watch the ballgame with him."

Grandpa dozes; so does baby. The ballgame continues. Time passes. So do other things.

Suddenly, Grandpa is awakened by the realization that his new Izods are soaked! The same Izods he cautioned the store not to make the inseam too short or he wouldn't pay for them. The same Izods that nearly cost the family cat his life for jumping on 'em with sharp claws.

His mind is jarred in the brief moment of realization.

"My God! Somebody pulled the plug in Lake Sinclair!" he says to himself as he inspects and verifies it.

Son-in-law expresses dutiful concern.

"Darn, Henry! I'm sorry about that. Here let me—"

"No problem, Jeff. No problem at all. Nature, you know. And hey! Look at that!" he says standing up with Lake Sinclair on his lap. "Man! The kid's got some kidneys. No kidney problem with this fella', Jeff!"

So, what do you do with grandchildren? Perhaps Otto von Bismarck answered it best and simplest when he said:

"You can do anything with children if you only play with them."

Teenage Marriages Don't Always Fail

This story is so true it almost flirts with fiction. It has darted across my mind on occasion for more than fifteen years.

She was beautiful, Karol was. Still is, in fact. She could have stepped right off the cover of *Seventeen,* although she was only sixteen at the time. Everybody in our town loved Karol, myself included. Her zest for living was torrid and contagious. Daddies pray for a daughter like Karol.

She was fourteen when I first met her and for the next two years I watched her grow and came to love her as my own. My own daughter was eight, but a miniature Karol in my eyes. My son was a classmate of Karol's and they were close friends. They enjoyed a beautiful friendship.

Karol had everything going for her. She was an excellent student, very popular, radiantly beautiful (still is), a majorette, a class officer, and worshiped by Robert, football hero and steady boyfriend, the only one she ever had. He was eighteen and a senior, the recipient of many honors for his gridiron exploits. It was an accepted fact that Robert and Karol would marry.

Storybook stuff so far, right? Handsome, athletic Robert and beautiful Karol. The ingredients from which America is made. Church and Sunday school? Every Sunday.

But then, the bubble burst.

I heard about it on a Saturday morning from a woman named Clara, and the news she was spreading was as unexpected as my next line.

"Have you heard about Karol? She's pregnant!"

My initial impulse was to hit Clara in the mouth. If you knew Clara, you'd know why. She'd rather spread bad news than win the Irish Sweepstakes, shoot a hole-in-one or lose forty pounds. The woman would walk through the Okefenokee Swamp in her last pair of pantyhose to deliver bad news. I'm sure that had she been in Massachusetts the night of April 18, 1775, she'd have been at least eight furlongs ahead of Paul Revere.

My second impulse was to throw up. My third was to find Karol, put my arms around her, and assure her I loved her. I did none of these. Instead, I eased into the back booth of a local cafe, ordered a cup of unwanted coffee, and cried. Golf? Not that day.

Karol's daddy took the easy way out. He went on a three-day, rip-roaring, to-hell-with-everybody drunk. It didn't help. When he sobered up his little girl was still pregnant.

So what do you do? Throw her into a dumpster and write her off as no good? Hustle her off to the abortion mill? Love her; love her to death because if she ever needed a helping hand. . .

I sat in church next morning, alone, and listened to the prelude. I thought about Karol and glanced repeatedly at her empty seat. But not for long. Shortly, she eased in between the pews and occupied it, alone. She was about ten feet away.

She smiled and nodded. I forced one of each in return. Karol knew that I knew. Then she bowed her head and prayed. Me, too. I prayed that the only time she would lower her head would be in prayer.

The girl never looked more radiant. Not on the sidelines of the football field, out front strutting to marching music, or dominating the stage at a beauty pageant, familiar turf to her. Had she made the slightest wiggle with a little finger I'd have been at her side in a wink. She didn't. Karol was going it alone, almost. Alone? I've never seen anyone so alone.

I could hear muted whispers. Clara had done her job well, as always. Telling Clara bad news is like striking a match to black powder. Made me wonder what she might have told the wise men about the Virgin Mary.

I mouthed the first song, mumbled my way through the responsive reading, and probably put something in the collection plate. I passed up the second song to remove a beam from my eye. The sermon? I confess, I never heard it. My mind was some ten feet to my left.

It was Communion Sunday. When my turn came I walked to the altar rail, knelt, and closed my eyes. I heard the rustle of dresses and cracking knee joints as others came. Then, I felt a small, smooth hand ease into mine. She whispered softly, "I love you, Mr. Whaley." I countered with the best I had at the time. "I love you too, Karol. I'm glad you're here."

Missed the sermon? I think not.

We broke bread and drank wine together before returning to the pew. We sat together and she squeezed my hand through the closing prayer. I wished that the minister had prayed longer.

Does my story end there? Hardly. That's only part one.

The Communion service was more than 15 years ago. Why tell the story? You just never know; maybe it needs to be told. Why? Because Robert and Karol and their two beautiful children are shining examples that life doesn't necessarily have to end with a teenage pregnancy out of wedlock. Rather, it could be a beginning.

Yes, they married, Karol had her baby, and she and Robert are so much in love today that it makes me feel good all over just to see them, which I do quite regularly. They faced their responsibilities head-on and have a beautiful marriage.

Karol could still compliment the cover of *Seventeen,* and

handsome Robert is a good, hard-working husband and father and a real asset to this community.

I saw Karol and Robert less than a month ago. I wish my friend at the grocery store could have seen them, too. And Clara. Good ol' Clara. Friend, I'd walk through the Okefenokee Swamp in my tuxedo to get her and have her come take a look.

They're beautiful and happy, and very much in love.

Part 8

A Sentimental Journey

Memories! How I love them! In fact, I get real sentimental when I think of such things as playin' marbles with my friends, punchin' holes in a biscuit with my one clean finger, gigglin' in church and school with my friends.

Then there's the home place, the home town, the family doctor, my first girlfriend, Mama and Daddy.

Some of it's changed, and some of it hasn't. But the memories and the feelings are still for real.

Remember the Other Heroes, Too

How many words have been written commemorating Memorial Day? Millions? Incalculable but, no matter, still insufficient.

From the smallest weekly gazette to the giant *New York Times,* every year writers try to portray the meaning of this day in a slightly different light. They (we) try new slants and improve on old ones, but still with one collective purpose in mind, to pay homage to an almost anonymous army of soldiers, sailors, and marines who made the supreme sacrifice for America. They gave their lives, and they did it for you and me, strangers that we were to them.

War breeds heroes, and America has been richly blessed

with many. Men will do, and have done, almost impossible and unbelievable things, and with no thought of heroism or recognition, when threatened with loss of liberty.

But let us remember this: there are degrees of death that only those who have experienced it can really know. They, too, should be remembered and honored on this day. Not one American ever died in battle who didn't leave casualties behind at home.

Like the mother who hung a gold star in her front window in 1943. She died as she stood there, not completely, but she died to a degree that only she can ever know. And she still dies a little every day. The hurt she feels gnawing at her insides is just as real as the hurt that comes from a bullet wound in Germany, a deadly hand grenade in the South Pacific, a bayonet wound in Korea, or a napalm burn in Vietnam.

Like the wife whose husband slept in mosquito-infested jungles of the South Pacific or the cold and frozen turf in Germany, until it came: "I regret to inform you that your husband . . ." is the way the cold and official telegram began in 1944. And the next phrase cut like a surgeon's scalpel, ". . . has been killed in action." She died a little every night when she turned off the light, lay in bed, and reached in vain for a husband and father who wasn't there—and hadn't been for what, to her, seemed an eternity. She lay in bed, night after night, confused and frustrated by a monster called "war." Yes, she cried, and died, every night.

Like the father, fishing pole in hand, who trudged down to the fish pond, alone, where he and his boy "used to catch 'em by the dozens." And he died a little every time he baited his hook, his thoughts not really concerned with such mundane things as bream, perch, and trout, but rather a ship in the cold and unfamiliar waters of the North Atlantic, an island in the steamy regions of the South Pacific, a river in Germany, a hill in Korea, or a rice paddy in Vietnam. The cork bobbles, once, twice, then disappears. He doesn't even notice. It really doesn't matter anymore. The war took his boy, his fishing buddy, and he dies a little more every day.

Like the children—what about the children? They died a

little, too, each time they asked, "Mommy, when is Daddy coming home?" And Mommy died with them each of the thousand times she answered, "I don't really know, honey. Soon, I hope, very soon."

And the casualty list goes on and on, the list of that breed of heroes known as surviving friends and relatives; the sweethearts, brothers, sisters, grandparents, and friends. Heroes. They are heroes just as surely as their men who slept in places unfit for a pig, ate rations they wouldn't have thrown out to a mongrel dog, and wore clothes, tattered, torn, and dirty that they wouldn't have given to a charity drive at home.

It's called the ravages of war and all involved, directly or indirectly, die to a degree when caught up in the vast vacuum of it, the only difference being the degree of death. And some become walking wounded, permanently crippled, when the unwanted and dreaded telegram comes: "I regret to inform you . . . killed in action."

Certainly, we pause each year to honor those who died on the battlefield. But it seems to me that we might also remember and honor those who died, but not completely, along with them. Surely they are heroes, too.

Falling Rain Brings Back Warm Memories

I don't remember who wrote "The Best Things in Life Are Free," but he was a wise songwriter. Remember? "The sun, the moon . . ."

Great, but he left out something: rain, rain on a tin roof. It should have been included. I know something about rain on a tin roof.

On a Monday night not long ago, it was raining so hard I could hardly wait to crawl in bed when I arrived home shortly after midnight. Looking forward to listening to the raindrops making sleep music on the air conditioner not more than two feet from my head, I cracked the window a couple of inches so I could hear it better.

The hard rain falling on the air conditioner took me back to my boyhood. I go back there a lot, and my latest trip in the rain was beautiful.

As a boy I knew the pleasure of sleeping under a tin roof with hard rain falling. I knew the bonus of being curled up and buried in a feather mattress as I did it. And the sheer joy of waking up on a cold and rainy Saturday morning in January to the realization that I didn't have to get out of bed and go to school.

Lord, I feel sorry for any child who grows up with the void of never having experienced at least one cold and rainy night in a feather mattress under a tin roof. (Please note that I said "in" a feather mattress. Any impostor who says he's slept "on" a feather mattress just ain't, because you can't.)

Remember the bedtime routine? Remember how you took your pillow and held it close to the fireplace until you could smell it scorching? Remember how you then ran hell-bent for bed, dived in under a ton of quilts, hugged that warm pillow like a long-lost lover, and disappeared into that feather mattress? And once there, if you moved an inch right or left, you froze? Oh, let it rain.

Remember what awaited you next morning? The coldest linoleum floor this side of Alaska and you had to cross it in your bare feet to start a fire in the fireplace. Bedroom slippers? Who had any?

I know about those little houses out back, too. You think Herschel Walker can run a fast forty-yard dash? You should have been in Powelton, Georgia, in the early thirties. My grandpa still holds the record.

Then there was the matter of washing your face and hands before breakfast. Simple. Just turn on the hot water, right? Not so fast, son. First there was the little matter of going to the well and drawing a bucket of water. Then, if you wanted hot water, Grandma would heat it on the wood stove in her kitchen while Bruno, the cat, and Scrappy, the dog, warmed their bellies. And Grandma sang. Grandma always sang.

At night the procedure was the same, except that instead of pouring the hot water in a washpan you dumped it in a foot tub, and squatted like a Filipino native to get your bath in front of the fireplace. Of course, you first had to convince

Bruno and Scrappy that you had first priority. And heaven help you if a hot coal popped out on you.

Memories. Lord, do I have memories.

The rain, the tin roof, the feather mattress were all bonuses. But there were pitfalls, too. And I remember some of them.

Like, did you ever have a cotton pickin' hog step on your foot on a cold and rainy morning? Ever walk through a wet and soggy lot to get to the cow barn? Ever had a cow slap you in the face on a cold morning with a wet, cocklebur-matted tail? Ever had one kick over a bucket of milk when you were half finished milking? Pitfalls.

But there were more pluses, too. Tell me this: is there anything warmer on a cold morning than putting your cheek next to a cow's belly? And did you ever wonder how the cow felt when you reached under to milk her? Who knows, maybe that's why the cow jumped over the moon.

Cold rain, tin roofs, feather mattresses, tons of quilts, warm pillows, that's what memories are made of.

One Clean Finger and Ragged Britches

It's funny how one simple act can bring back so many memories. And while I don't live in the past, neither do I have any regrets for my childhood.

I was raised poor, I guess, but nobody bothered to tell me so I never really knew it. Of course, there are all kinds of ways to be poor. A family can have mountains of money, but no love, and wallow in the muck and mire of poverty. But I have great memories of a beautiful childhood and a wonderful mother and father who did without so their little boy wouldn't know the pitfalls of poverty.

A little incident that happened in the obscure village of Register last week triggered my childhood memories, if for only a little while.

I was en route to Savannah and stopped at a little country store to buy a Coke, some Vienna sausages, and saltine crackers. There are times, you know, when only such delicacies will satisfy.

After making my purchases, I went outside to eat them off the hood of my car. While partaking, I heard one heck of an argument and turned to see three dirty little boys yelling at the top of their lungs. Being a nosy character, I ambled over to see what was going on.

I was amazed and pleased to see what it was they were in such a heated argument about. Marbles! They were shooting marbles, something I hadn't seen done in years. The argument was incidental. I offered to buy them Cokes, and that ended it anyway.

After leaving my outdoor restaurant, I thought about the game all the way to Savannah. Marbles. Funny how the meaning of words and phrases changes with the years. Forty years ago if you had told my parents, "Bo has lost his marbles," their only concern would have been that the preacher's son had been playing for keeps. (There were only two ways to play marbles: for keeps or for fun. And the preacher's son just wasn't allowed to play for keeps.)

Today, however, should you inform a mother that her son had "lost his marbles," she would immediately place an emergency call to the family shrink.

For those of you who may have been unfortunate enough to glide through adolescence without experiencing a good game of marbles, you may have missed a bit of what America was all about in the thirties. Heck, in those days a thirteen-year-old boy without a sack full of marbles was as out of touch with reality as one today without a tape player. His prized possession? His agate, of course. (If you don't know what one is, ask your daddy. He'll know if he's over fifty.)

The worst fight I ever saw was between Edward Coogle and Buttercup Hill, in Oglethorpe, over the ownership of an agate. I don't remember who won the fight but Doyce Ellis and I won all the marbles. We walked home with a pocket full, leaning so far to the right we looked like two wagons with broken springs and sounding like hail hitting a tin roof. (When I got home I hid mine under the church steps next door to our house. Like I said, preachers' sons weren't allowed to play for keeps.)

Marbles had no value. They were a status symbol. When I was in the sixth and seventh grades in Oglethorpe, there was no way I was going to school without a pocket full of marbles. My morning routine was: eat breakfast, grab my books, reach under the church steps and load my pocket, and walk to school looking like a wagon with a broken spring and sounding like hail on a tin roof.)

My best friend, Doyce Ellis, was the best marble shooter I ever saw. He lived only two doors from me and we shot marbles every day.

Two distinct signs identified the dedicated marble shooters: a hole in the right knee of his britches and dirty, raw knuckles on his right hand. No way to play marbles on the pro tour like Doyce and I did without ripped britches and raw knuckles.

When the marble game ended, Doyce and I always followed the same ritual: he'd go home with me or I'd go home with him for "refreshments," which usually consisted of leftover biscuits, sweet potatoes, and sausage or ham. To this day I can't recall having eaten anything that tasted better.

Now then, we didn't just grab that cold biscuit and start eating. No, sir! First, we held it tightly with our dirty left hand cupped around it. Then, we slowly and methodically took our dirty right forefinger and poked a hole in it, being particularly careful that the forefinger went straight and true, about two-thirds of the way in.

Then we took the syrup bottle, poured real cane syrup in the hole, and waited for a minute to allow the syrup to saturate the inner regions of that biscuit. Experts, which we were, could do it and never spill a drop. Ummmm, syrup and biscuit, cold sweet potato, cold country ham or sausage. How're you gonna' top that? Especially if you're two cold and hungry professional marble shooters?

Many times after I was grown I heard my daddy say that Doyce and I had but one clean finger the entire time we lived in Oglethorpe—our right forefinger.

I still eat sausage, biscuit, and syrup for breakfast every morning. The difference now is that they aren't my mama's biscuits and I don't poke holes in them with my finger any more. I think I'll just change that in the morning, though, and poke me a good hole and pour in the syrup.

My good marble-shooting friend Doyce can't be with me because he died a few years ago. But I can sit there, alone, and reflect on our good boyhood days together.

What the heck—I may even poke holes in two biscuits. I have the feeling Doyce would like that.

Why Are Things Always Funnier in Church and at School?

Why is it that things that happen in school and church are *always* funnier than any other place? I mean, we go into hysterics at church and school shenanigans that we wouldn't normally give a second grin to in other settings.

Like a growling stomach, for instance. Is there anything the least bit humorous about a growling stomach? There is in church and school. And let me ask you this: does a stomach *really* growl louder in church and school, or does it just seem that way? A lone housefly on a bald head can, and usually does, produce an identical reaction. Or a dropped song book, somebody singing the third verse while the entire congregation is singing the fourth, or maybe some soul standing while everybody else sits. Nothing sacrilegious or irreverent about any of these things. They're just funnier in church.

And I'm sure that the preacher must see things every Sunday morning from his lofty vantage point that test his composure. And teachers must view similar scenes in the classroom.

On a recent Sunday morning, for instance, I was privileged to partake of Holy Communion, one of the most sacred of Christian rituals, at my church with my daughter and her best friend, Lisa Brown, who drove from Macon to visit me and my mother. I was as proud as a peacock as I walked with my daughter to the communion table and knelt there with her by my side. In fact, I was so engrossed in being with her that I passed up the collection plate on my way down to the altar rail like it wasn't there. And we both had cold cash in our hands to deposit.

As we rose and walked back to our pew, Lisa reminded me of my error, detoured by the collection plate, and made a deposit for both of us. A youngster seated near the front thought that was about the funniest thing he'd seen since TV's Saturday morning cartoons. His mother failed to grasp the humor of the moment.

Here's a true story about Holy Communion that came to mind that Sunday morning as I sat in my pew at First United Methodist and waited for others to partake. I know it's true because I was there and witnessed it. I must have been about eleven at the time. It broke Doyce Ellis, my best friend, and me up.

The place was the Oglethorpe First Methodist Church (not yet United). My father, the Reverend W. W. Whaley, the pastor, was serving, and some six or seven little boys, about five or six years old, occupied the front pew, as always. One of them was Raymond Riddle, son of Dennis and Christine Riddle.

As my father methodically passed the unleavened bread (broken soda crackers) and wine (Welch's grape juice), he repeated the words so familiar to all who commune: " 'Take, eat, this is my body which was broken for you.' . . . Likewise, after supper, He took the cup and said, 'Drink, for this is my blood which was spilled for you. . . .' And now, arise, and go in peace." Raymond watched and listened with more than a passing interest.

When about the third table had finished communion, Raymond stood up, reached in his pocket, and withdrew a double handful of bubble gum. He then moved along the front pew, dispensing his bubble gum as he went, repeating these words, "Take this and chew it. It is for you . . . and you . . . and you."

Dennis and Christine Riddle, seated some three or four pews away, died a double death. My father saw what was happening and immediately moved to their pew and whispered something in their ear before returning to the communion table to finish serving.

After the service, my mother asked my father what he had whispered to Raymond's parents.

"I just told them to stay where they were because I thought Raymond's act of serving bubble gum to his friends was one of the most beautiful and unselfish gestures I had ever witnessed in my ministry, and to *please* not punish him in any way."

Yes, things have a tendency to be extremely funny in church. On the other hand, I guess it just depends on how you view them.

As for little Raymond Riddle? I know for a fact that he grew up to be one of the prime leaders in Oglethorpe's First Methodist Church (now United)—and my father loved him.

"After all," he later said to Raymond's mother and father at a church reunion, "who am I to say that Raymond and his front pew friends weren't partaking of Holy Communion that memorable Sunday morning in Oglethorpe in 1938? The soda crackers and grape juice were merely symbols. Why not bubble gum?"

Memory of My First Date Lingers, Unfortunately

I was in a flower shop when I noticed a boy buy what was obviously his first corsage. I surmised that he'd rather be fishing or shooting basketball.

The modern-day Huckleberry Finn, clad in T-shirt, jeans, and Keds, selected carnations and moved to a remote corner of the shop to mull over the message he'd eventually write on the card. Some things are very private, you know. I wouldn't have peeped had I been a CIA agent, but I was dying to know.

I watched him leave with his purchase and get into the car with his mother, who had been waiting outside. I imagined the conversation that might have taken place between them before he went into the flower shop. The exchange could have gone something like this:

"What kind of corsage are you getting for Ramona, son?"

"What kind of what?"

"Corsage. Ramona must have a corsage to wear to the dance. She'd feel undressed without one. What color is her dress? It has to match her dress."

"Aw, Mom, does she really have to wear one of them things?"

"Certainly, Henry. Your sister will be wearing one."

"Well, that's different. She's fat."

"What's that got to do with it?"

"Well, Ramona just don't need one. And besides, how's she gonna dance all strapped down in one of them things?"

I guess some things are etched in your memory forever. First bicycle, first kiss, first grade, first beer, first sergeant, first wife, and last, but not least, that first date. I remember mine like it was 46 years ago.

Her name was Ann Cornell. If she had a middle name, I never knew it. Probably Venus. Lord, she was beautiful! Was I nervous? Honey, compared to me, Don Knotts was a walking, living, breathing Valium.

The year was 1943. I was a cadet at Georgia Military College (GMC). Ann was a freshman at Georgia State College for Women (GSCW). (I'm not using her real name. She has five brothers who know where I live, and the smallest one couldn't walk through double doors without turning sideways and bending down.)

Ann was tall, shapely, and just generally the most beautiful girl on or off campus in Milledgeville. Beauty runs in the Cornell family as evidenced by her two nieces who live right here in Dublin. Dolls, they're just living dolls.

I first laid eyes on Ann Cornell in Tommy's Soda Shop, gathering place and a required off-campus course for all "Jimmys and Jessies," as the cadets at GMC and the girls at GSCW were called. Classes met there every afternoon with double sessions on Saturday and Sunday. Field trips to the Martin Theater next door were offered as electives. Everybody took that course. What the heck, it was the only place you could take a Jessie and be in the dark. The campus had more lights than Atlanta Stadium and more guards than

Reidsville State Prison. And each dorm had a live-in warden.

It was a Saturday afternoon, and I let a perfectly good chocolate milkshake ruin right under my nose after Ann walked into Tommy's. My roommate, Al Whitfield, lost a vanilla. If she'd spoken to me, I'd have jumped in mine. She didn't.

I practically broke Al's ribs with my elbow when I punched him. "Al! Who in the world is that? Do you know her?" I asked.

"What do you think? If I knew her, would I be sitting in this booth with you?" he shot back.

"It ought to be against the law for a girl to be that pretty," I said.

I paid for my untouched shake and left, but not before getting the girl's name from Tommy. I'd have blackmailed him to get it.

"Her name's Ann Cornell. Freshman. Lives in Beeson Hall," he told me.

"She goin' with anybody?" I asked.

"Never seen her with anybody, Bo," he said.

"O.K. Thanks, Tommy."

Al heard the entire exchange between Tommy and me.

"She's probably goin' steady with some out-of-towner," he groaned.

"Yeah, you're probably right. Like Clark Gable or Errol Flynn," I said. "But I'm gonna' call her anyway."

Al made no reply. He just laughed, and laughed, and laughed.

I could hardly wait for 7:00 P.M. That's when we were allowed to use the telephone in Vinson Hall. I nervously made the call to Beeson Hall and asked to speak to Ann Cornell. Details aren't important, but the fact that she accepted my invitation to go to the movie the next afternoon is.

To say I was ecstatic is a gross understatement. I actually had a date with Ann Cornell! The news spread through the halls of dear ol' Vinson. I was an instant hero. Gable and Flynn would just have to wait.

I was up and at 'em long before the bugler next morning. I

had already shined my shoes twice and shaved three times
when he tooted the first note of reveille. My date with Ann
wasn't until 1:00 P.M., but I was all set at 6:30 A.M.

I walked around all morning with a silly grin on my face
and shook my watch every ten minutes. I combed my hair
every five and changed shirts three times. After all, I
couldn't walk in the lobby and ask for Ann Cornell in a
sweaty shirt.

At 12:30 P.M., I began the walk to GSCW. (Yes, we walked
on dates back in 1943. I entered Beeson Hall right on the
button, 1:00 P.M. and asked for Ann Cornell, proud as a
peacock.

The warden at the desk made it all seem so routine when
she called upstairs, shouting, "Cornell! Your date's here!"

After that, I watched the stairs like a sentry. Actually I
was Rhett Butler, and Scarlett O'Hara never descended a
staircase as beautifully as did Ann Cornell minutes later.
There should have been chamber music.

Ecstasy, pure ecstasy, was the feeling as we walked to the
Martin Theater. I hoped that the entire cadet corps would
see me, especially Al Whitfield.

I saw the line of Jimmys and Jessies at the ticket window
as we approached the theater. Three things you could depend on: death, taxes, and a line at the Martin. We joined in
and I stood tall and proud.

So much for the ecstasy; now for the agony.

When my turn came to buy tickets, I reached in what had
to be the deepest and emptiest pocket in Milledgeville,
Georgia.

I had taken such pains with my shoes, shirt, and hair, but
had neglected one important thing: money! I had no money,
and there I stood with the most beautiful girl in the world.
Dumb! Just plain dumb.

Ann bailed me out and bought the tickets. I could have
died right there in front of the Martin Theater. I think I did,
and in a sweaty shirt.

I'm sure there was a movie on the screen. I really don't
remember. It really didn't matter because I was sitting next
to Ann Cornell.

By the way, Ann, wherever you are, honey, I owe you fifty

cents. I'll pay. I'll gladly pay if you just won't tell those five big brothers of yours.

No Sympathy for Life's Common Ailments

Want to get scared out of your boxers, baby? What would you think if you went to your doctor with a runny nose and he suggested you visit a rhinologist?

A rhinologist? Where does he practice? Grant Park Zoo? Disney World? How was I to know the guy is a nose specialist?

Try this one on, Kildare. You turn in for "tests." Six days later you are confronted by your consultant, the guy who puts all the test results together and gives you the final evaluation. He peers through horn-rimmed glasses and John L. Lewis eyebrows for an eternity, plus eighteen seconds, and finally says, "Well, we have determined that you have spastic colitis and—"

Spastic colitis! What do you do? You panic, turn over the bedpan, and break out in a cold sweat, gasping, "Just give it to me straight, Doc! How much time do I have left?"

Spastic colitis? What he was telling you was that you are nervous and it causes the smooth muscles in your colon to tighten up. So there you lay, foaming at the mouth. A confirmed spastic!

However, being treated by a rhinologist for spastic colitis is not without advantages. At least you get sympathy from friends and neighbors. After all, who's gonna' sympathize with a nervous guy with a runny nose?

You get no sympathy with common ailments. You gotta' be fancy.

Want to be the hero of Willacoochee? Take acupuncture treatments. The Atkinson County Fair Association will give you top billing next October and children will toss peanuts and bananas at you.

How much sympathy would you get if you told a friend your blood wasn't clotting properly? Maybe a "Hmmmmmm" or an "Oh, I see."

Tell him you've got agranulocytosis, and he'll call Jerry Lewis to arrange a telethon—and make a donation.

Bad blood just won't get it, Homer.

Never indicate that you simply had your heartbeat checked. You can buy a stethoscope at the five and dime. No, strike that, the twenty-five and fifty, and do that yourself. Come on strong. Tell the coffee table you had a ballistiocardiograph and watch their eyes bulge!

Grandma Was Two Generations Early

Remember how she used to churn, boil clothes in a wash pot, scrub shirts and underwear on a washboard, pick blackberries, and make homemade jelly? She never missed a chore, but she complained every day of an ailment that generated little sympathy. Remember?

"What's the matter, Grandma? You sick?"

"Yeah, I sure am, son."

"What's the matter?"

Shootin' pains! I got shootin' pains."

Shootin' pains! She had 'em all her life but I never knew what they were. Still don't.

She'd have given a week's egg money just to take one electroencephalograph. It would have provided all the ammunition she needed for church meetings and family reunions. It never happened because Dr. Cooper went no further than tongue depressor, thermometer, and stethoscope. Always gave the same diagnosis.

"Shootin' pains, Miss Jessie."

Mrs. Byrd Williamson, who lived across the street, had the same symptoms and the same doctor. She received the same examination as Grandma but came away with a different diagnosis:

"That ol' mess!"

No sympathy for Mrs. Williamson. Just once, she would have settled for "shootin' pains."

But Dr. Cooper was something of a psychologist as well as a GP. He gave both Grandma and Mrs. Williamson "braggin' rights."

He always told Grandma that her "shootin' pains" were

"acute." So, what did he do for Mrs. Williamson? He assured her that "that ol' mess" was "chronic."

Not an electroencephalograph by any means, but more of a sympathy producer than gout and shingles.

It seems that a hypochondriac, in listing all his complaints to his doctor, added that he was also losing his hearing.

"It's getting so bad, Doc, that I can't even hear myself coughing."

The doctor scribbled off a quick prescription.

"Will this improve my hearing?" he asked.

"No," replied the doctor, "but it will make you cough much louder."

Things I Wish I Could Have Done

I once wrote a column about the places I've been, the things I've done, the people I've met. It wasn't long before people were asking me, "What about the things you wish you could have done? I recall many things I'd like to have done but know I never will."

The question got me to thinking. So here are some of the places I've never been; people I've never met, and things I've never done, but always wanted to:

- I wish I could have eaten fried chicken with Colonel Sanders—and watched him lick his fingers.
- I wish I could watch Mr. Goodwrench give my Mercury a tune-up.
- I wish I could attend just one wedding reception where club sandwiches and king-size Cokes are served.
- I wish I could dance, just once, with Dolly Parton, up close, to the "Tennessee Waltz."
- I wish I could have met Kilroy somewhere along the World War II trail. I never did. Everywhere I went Kilroy had already been and left.
- I wish I could walk in a laundromat, bid fifty-one-dol-

lars on a dirty T-shirt and take it away from some Madison Avenue guy that had just bid fifty-dollars on it.

- I wish I could find out once and for all what's behind "The Green Door."
- I wish I could engage in a lengthy conversation with Howard Cosell, on a day when he had acute laryngitis.
- I wish I could board a Greyhound bus, sit behind the wheel, and say to the driver, "Relax, fella'. Leave the driving to me."
- I wish I had the nerve to walk up to a ticket agent at Delta's Gate 66 and say, "Sorry, but I ain't ready yet."
- I wish I could take a head count just to see if Jerry Falwell really does have a majority.
- I wish I could watch Jane Fonda and Madelyn Murray O'Hare mud-wrestle.
- I wish I could watch Perry Como sleep just to see if I could tell the difference.
- I wish I could get reservations for twelve at Nikolai's Roof in Atlanta for 8:00 P.M.—and cancel at 7:45.
- I wish I could have interviewed Lee Harvey Oswald in the Dallas jail and he'd told me the truth. I'd have asked, "Will you tell me all you know about a guy named Jack Ruby?"
- I wish I could book Miss Clairol on my radio show and ask her this, "Tell me, honey, do you or don't you?"
- I wish I knew which twin has the Toni.
- I wish I could hear just one politician say, "Well, to tell you the truth, I'm runnin' for the office because I need the cotton pickin' salary."
- I wish I could ask Gaylord Perry of the Seattle Mariners, "Gaylord, do you or don't you?"
- I wish I could hear some character blurt out from the back of the church, "Hold it! You're dang right I got reasons why they shouldn't be lawfully joined together!"
- I wish I could watch a beer drinking contest between Lewis Grizzard and a fella I know named Edward. No contest. I'd spot Grizzard a case of long-neck Buds and he'd still lose.
- I wish, just once, I would dial a wrong number in Cal-

ifornia and get Bo Derek on the phone instead of Buddy
Hackett.
- I wish I could have ridden "up front" with Casey Jones.
- I wish I could see Rock City, but not on the roof of some
North Georgia barn.
- I wish I could meet Mr. Maxwell House and ask him,
"What's wrong with the last drop, Mr. House?"
- I wish I could identify the individual who came up with
this bumper sticker and ask him if he's ever played golf
with me: "If You Think I'm a Bad Driver; You Ought to
See Me Putt!"
- But most of all, I wish I could hear my daddy preach
just one more time. That's what I really wish.

The Beauty of Imagination

I don't recall who said it but I like it: "Beauty lies in the eyes
of the beholder." It says an awful lot and prompted me to
give a great deal of thought to imagination. You see, without
it I could never have been Tom Mix or Hopalong Cassidy
and shot all those Indians; or Tarzan as I swung on that little
piece of rope in the back yard from the chinaberry tree to
the roof of the garage; or Jesse James when I was holding up
all those trains in South Georgia back in the thirties; or
Babe Ruth when I stepped to the plate in that cow pasture in
Hancock County some forty years ago to await the first
pitch from Carl Hubbell (Allen Rainwater, really). No, and
my son, Joe, could never have been Davy Crockett here in
Dublin back in '53 when he donned that coonskin cap and
hunted bears all up and down Duncan Street with his ever-
present bear hunting partner (and baby sitter) Willene
Talley. Yep, imagination can indeed be fun—and was for me
over a recent Labor Day weekend. It went like this.
    It has come to my attention more and more in recent
years just how many vacant and abandoned country homes
there are. I challenge you to drive fifty miles from your
home, in any direction, and not see at least a hundred. I did

just that when I headed south to Lyons, Georgia, and a little white house on North Victory Drive occupied by a lady who thinks I hung the moon. You see, she has quite an imagination, too!

The day proved to be even greater than I anticipated. Mother and I talked about everything from politics to grandsons. We ate barbecue and potato salad and drank iced tea. We laughed a lot—and reminisced a lot. I didn't want to leave. I never do. And . . . more important than that, she didn't want me to, either. But all good things must come to an end, and this day was no exception.

As I drove north from Lyons toward Dublin, I seemed to notice more abandoned homes than usual; maybe it was because I had more time to look. At any rate, the recurring scene fascinated me, to the point where I pulled off the road, drove some hundred yards and stopped in front of an old house that probably hasn't known a human being well over thirty years—and won't for the next thirty. I sat in my car for a few minutes just looking and this is when my imagination began taking over. "The forming of a mental image of something not present," according to Webster.

I closed my car door and two suspicious squirrels darted behind the trunk of a giant oak tree in the front yard. Surely their great-great-great-great-grandfather had played in that same tree. To them, I was trespassing.

The sagging front porch was held up by two giant crutches in the form of withered and rotten two-by-fours accented by two huge wasp nests near the top. I took special notice of this. I could handle the squirrels, but I just plain don't mess around with wasps. I give them all the respect they deserve. I moved a few steps closer so that I could invade the living room visibly. I knew it would be there and it was. A fireplace. No way this house wouldn't have had a fireplace. I leaned against the door frame and let my imagination take a trip. I could almost see the old gentleman sitting there with a poker in his hand to stir the oak logs. In my mind's eye he was smoking a pipe, probably with Prince Albert tobacco. He would have lit it with a kitchen match taken from his mouth or a cup on the mantelpiece. His dog would move only when nudged by the old gentleman, or when a hot coal popped out without warning. In all probability, both the dog and his master would doze for a while before they retired, the dog outside, reluctantly, and the old man, willingly, in a feather bed upstairs.

My imagination wasn't quite through with me yet. I could almost smell the good country ham and hear an elderly lady singing, "Amazing Grace" or "The Old Rugged Cross." She would join her mate by the fireplace and either sew, churn, or do some other chores while he and the dog slept. She would keep singing, but a little softer. She would then turn in her Bible to a favorite passage and read it while she thought of her children, long since gone to make their way in the world—and their way back to the old homeplace regularly. That is what she and the old gentleman really lived for.

The old house was bare of paint and furniture, with the exception of one old broken rocker that lay on its side in one corner of the living room. It had a high back and also a broken seat to go along with the rocker. There were notches on the well-worn arms and I imagined that the old gentleman placed them there as he sat in the chair many hours contemplating the next day's chores—or the ones just completed. I would like to have translated those notches from thoughts to words, but my imagination just wouldn't go that far. If so, I probably would have experienced thoughts of children and grandchildren, of Sunday church and what the preacher had said, of too much rain, or not enough. Maybe a tear or two as he reflected on a son in Europe or the South Pacific as he glanced at the two stars hanging on a flag in the window, both blue, with an earnest prayer that neither would turn to gold overnight.

But that old rocking chair could have been many things. It could have been a throne where many years before the old gentleman, as a young man, had brought his queen to live with him, and eyed her proudly as she occupied it; it could have been an altar, too, where youngsters knelt at their mother's knee to offer their prayers to God before turning their backside to the warm fireplace for one last toasting before scrambling, barefoot, across the cold linoleum floor to feather beds. And it could have been a prison, too, for an elderly man or woman whose only crime was that of growing old—gracefully. In any event, I had the feeling that the now-still rocker could tell quite a story if only it could talk. Maybe it's better that it just lay mute and let my imagination do the talking.

For a little while I was the "beholder" and, thanks to my imagination, that old house once again became a home.

And it was beautiful.

Some Things Don't Change, but Most Do

Some time ago I went back to my home town of Lumpkin, Georgia. I was amazed at how little had changed at Clyde Richardson's store. About the only thing that's changed in the past forty-some years is the price of the merchandise. But Mr. Clyde's store is about the only thing that remains unchanged in downtown Lumpkin, with the exception of the Stewart County Courthouse. It remains the same and looks like it came right off the set of "To Kill a Mockingbird."

I drove slowly clockwise around the courthouse square, desperately searching for something, or someone, familiar from the early forties. I should have stayed at Richardson's store, for Holder's Cafe, where I have eaten the best hamburgers in the world, was gone. R. S. Wimberly's law office, where my daddy spent countless hours in conversation, was gone. Boyd Moon's True Blue Grocery, where I bought bubble gum and candy, was gone. The post office, where I used to send my requests home from college for a little spending money, and where Daddy mailed it to me, was gone. Thompson's Drug Store, where Elizabeth Mathis made the best cherry Cokes known to a fifteen-year-old boy, was gone. So was Sib Fort's Standard Station where Sonny Butts used to drink R. C. Colas by the case, and the bank, Pugh's Grocery, Barr's Drug Store, Charles Troutman's Pool Room, and the theater—all gone.

A big lump came in my throat when I saw that empty, run-down, and deserted theater building where Hopalong

Cassidy, Roy Rogers, Bob Steele, Wild Bill Elliott, Ken
Maynard, and Gene Autry fought Indians and cattle rustlers
every Saturday afternoon—and always won. It was also the
building in which Phyllis Watson became engaged eight or
nine times every Saturday afternoon, on the back row, seat
two. Phyllis worked in shifts, and a fella' had to get there
early to get in line. Phyllis's theater seat should be in the
theater hall of fame. She was the Dolly Parton of the early
forties in Lumpkin.

But there was a bright light to be seen on my drive around
the square: the Singer Company, where men sat for hours
and shelled peanuts, was still there on the corner. Sam
Singer, Jr., was my best friend and is the young man who
developed an 1850s community showplace just outside of
Lumpkin, in Westville.

I left downtown Lumpkin and drove nine miles to Providence Canyon, a state park now. I went there to visit the
church that sits on the rim of the canyon, Providence United
Methodist Church (established in 1859). My father pastored
the church from 1939 to 1943. It was known as an "afternoon appointment," and after Sunday afternoon church services all the boys in the church would play in the canyon
while the grown-ups stayed behind and talked about places
like Germany, Africa, Italy, Midway, Bougainville, Salerno,
Normandy. It was known as World War II.

I stood and looked at Providence Church. My heart was
heavy because it is surrounded now by a barricade and
church services are only held every fifth Sunday. I thought
to myself, "With all the sinning that goes on in the world,
here we have a church that's idle most of the time. A
shame."

I left the church and walked to the rim of the canyon,
looked down inside it for a few minutes, threw a rock in it
just for old time's sake, and drove back to Lumpkin.

On the way back I stopped briefly at what used to be
Stewart County High School. It now looks unkempt, unat-
tractive and, like those of us who graduated from there
"magna thank the laude" over forty years ago, is showing its
age. I didn't tarry because the appearance of the building
tarnished the beautiful memories I stored up when a student

there. And there is nothing worse than good times remembered in misery.

The home of Frank Singer is one block from the old school. His daughter, Marilena, was a classmate and great friend of mine. My daddy hunted quail all over southwest Georgia with Mr. Frank. I stopped my car in front of the house, which is now deserted and neglected. I thought about Mr. Frank and the day I attended his funeral in 1942. He was a completely devout nonconformist, the only person I've ever seen buried in pajamas (at his request). They were light blue, and he looked completely relaxed. There was also a package of Lucky Strike cigarettes and a box of matches in the pocket (again, at his request). My father officiated at his funeral service, and Mr. Frank's unusual request that he be buried in pajamas makes a lot more sense to me now that it did in 1942.

I had seen enough of my former town and had kept my promise of more than forty years. So I headed out of town in the direction of Richland. But on the way out I had a last smile as I drove by the old home place of the Warren brothers, Louie and Grady. Like my old school building, Providence Church, and Frank Singer's house, the Warren house was in bad shape. The Warren brothers long ago departed this world, so why did I smile as I drove by? Memories, friend, memories.

You see, like John Houseman says of Smith-Barney—Louie and Grady made money the old-fashioned way: they were bootleggers!

Bo Whaley has won twenty-one awards as a columnist for the Dublin, Georgia, Courier Herald. He speaks to more than 200 audiences each year, hosts a morning radio talk show, is the author of *Rednecks and Other Bonafide Americans*, ''and loafs a lot.''